DIRTY WORK

BROKEN MAGIC
BOOK 4

DEVON MONK

ODD
HOUSE
PRESS

DIRTY WORK

USA Today Bestselling author Devon Monk's final book in her fast, magic-fueled, urban fantasy adventure series. Death and Life magic, enemies-to-brothers, chosen family, and a battle—and a choice—that will change the shape of the world. *Brand new novel bursting with Heart, Snark, and glorious Ass-kicking.*

Shame Flynn is a Death magic user who has seen some shit. He and Life magic user, Terric Conley have spent the last three years keeping a lid on magic while hunting down the criminals and monsters bent on using it for revenge.

So far, they've managed to hide the magical hot spots from the world. But now their very smart, ex-magic user friends, Allie and Zayvion Beckstom-Jones are asking questions. Questions about magic Shame and Terric can't answer if they want to keep their friends safe.

But when Allie and Zayvion's three-year-old daughter disappears, there is no time for secrets. No time for subterfuge. There is only time for justice.

The search for the missing girl triggers powerful enemies, ancient magic, and dangerous truths. Truths that will make or break Shame and Terric's lives, and the lives of the people they would die for.

Dirty Work

Copyright © 2023 by Devon Monk

ISBN: 9781939853417

Publisher: Odd House Press

Cover Art: Lou Harper Cover Affairs

Interior Design: Odd House Press

For my family and all the readers looking for a little more magic

CHAPTER 1

The gargoyle had very large teeth. He pulled his lips back in a snarl and tipped his wide head side to side, giving every one of those teeth its moment in the spotlight.

I, Shamus Flynn, did not like being flat on my back with a deadly beast growling down at me like I was lunch.

Luckily, I knew this particular deadly beast.

"Hey, Stoney," I said, blinking up at the gargoyle and the clear night sky he'd just dropped out of. "What's shaking, buddy?"

Stone's growl turned into a watery burble as his triangle ears swiveled forward, then toward the noise coming from the house.

Party noise. From the party-goers saying their goodbyes and see-ya-laters at the front of the house.

Was there a reason I was sneaking around the back of the Beckstrom-Jones's place? Yes. I'd been avoiding both of my besties for months now. Not just because I carried Death magic and had to do some killing every now and then to keep it happy.

The reason I'd been avoiding them was because Allie Beckstrom-Jones, and her hubby, Zayvion, were too damn smart for their own good.

Smart friends made for suspicious friends.

Suspicious friends got hurt.

The last thing I needed was either of them paying attention to what I and my Soul Complement, Terric Conley, had been doing in our off time.

Stone sniffed at my head, his breath hot and wet in my hair. I patted the side of the big lug's face. "It hasn't been that long, mate." I scratched behind his ears.

He shivered in pleasure and leaned into my hand, wings up and out like twin umbrellas, all the grumbles traded for vacuum cleaner sounds.

Happy sounds. Which was good. I never wanted to really piss off the big guy.

Stone was a rare bit of magic in the world now. The only magic-fueled creature in existence. He was Allie Beckstrom's pet and had become my goddaughter, Ramona's, guardian.

Apparently he'd also appointed himself the bouncer for this particular shindig.

"We good?" I asked giving his head one last pat. "'Cause I landed on a rock and my ass is killing me."

He leaned closer and glared, saucer eyes black and shot through with little sparks of light. He growled.

Then he picked up my hand and put it back on the top of his head.

I scratched, and he snorted and grumbled again, burbling like a broken toilet.

Complaining. He was bitching me out.

"Hey, now," I said. "It hasn't been that long since I've been here."

"It really has," a male voice said from somewhere over my shoulder.

Footsteps came my way, quiet on the stone pathway, even though the boots were big. There was a good reason for the size of those boots. They fit the man, all muscled six-feet-two of him, who stared down at me disapprovingly.

He was darker skinned than my own white-boy self, his tight black curls shaved close to his head, which only make his cheekbones and brown-gold eyes sharper. His lips were turned down in a scowl, his clean-shaven jaw clenched.

Sure, most people who knew him thought he was calm and cool. Zen. But I'd seen him tear people apart with his bare hands.

"Zayvion," I said.

Stone planted one big mitt on my chest and leaned, pushing all the air out of my lungs like I was some kind of kill he'd just bagged. "Nice weather we're having," I wheezed.

Zayvion Jones was my best friend in the world. He and I had grown up in the Authority, a now defunct secret magic society that had secretly taught secret ways to use magic, and secret ways to use magic to hurt people.

The Authority's main goal had been to keep bad guys from doing bad things with magic. Bad guys had, of course, found ways to do bad and worse things with magic and had used it to nearly destroy the world.

Good guys had found ways around the rules too.

The whole thing had led to a lot of battles, a lot of deaths, a lot of betrayals and revenge, yada-to-the-yada, and then magic got locked away for good.

No more powerful spells that moved faster than the eye could track. No more using magic and making someone else pay the price of pain for it.

No more magic for anything.

Good or bad.

My friends and I had paid the price to lock away magic.

In doing so, we'd lost friends and lovers. We'd died —I had died more than once—to shut the door on magic, slam the bars, stick it on a shelf so high, no living thing could touch it.

Zayvion knew about all that because he'd been there doing most of it.

But at the end...there at the *very* end, it had been Terric and me who shut magic down.

If we'd also cheated and left one little loophole that let just the two of us—Terric and me—still use magic? Well, no one needed to know that little secret.

Especially not my best friend, Mr. Zen, Mr. Perfect Zayvion Jones.

"Shamus." He crossed arms over his chest. "About time you showed your face. We expected you months ago."

"Invitation got lost in the mail."

Stone gasped a little hoot sound.

"We sent it via gargoyle. Pretty sure Stone handed it directly to you."

Stone leaned a little harder and stuck his face in my face. The teeth were back on display. He growled.

"Okay, fine. I got the invite. I just got busy."

"Too busy for friends? For family?"

"C'mon, Jones—Stoney, mate. Ease up. Can't talk. No air."

Stone just leaned a fraction more forward.

"Oh, fuuuck..."

Zayvion tugged on the gargoyle's ear. "Let him up. You did good, Stone."

"Good?" I groaned as Stone finally shifted away. "My ribs are crushed. He sat on me and crushed my actual bones."

"You're lucky it's only your ribs that are crushed. I told him to sit on your head if needed."

I pressed one hand to the grass and levered myself upward onto my knees. I made a big show of moving slowly and rubbing at my sides. "And you wonder why I don't visit."

Zay snorted. "Should I ask what took you so long?"

"Today's the party, right?"

"Yes. That's not what I'm talking about, and you know it."

He held my gaze long enough that if I'd been a better man, I might have felt guilty and looked away. Too bad for him I had never been a better man.

"You missed me," I cooed, batting my eyes.

One eyebrow ticked upward. There was violence in those eyes.

I really shouldn't push him.

So I did.

"Life's boring without me around. Old married Papa Beckstrom-Jones. Balancing the checking account, falling asleep in the recliner, dreaming of sensible vacations in sensible hotels with sensible views." I glanced at his feet. "And sensible shoes."

Jaw tick. Nostrils flared.

Good. An angry Zayvion was easy to distract.

Well, easier.

"You want to tell me what you're hiding, or would you like to wait for me to find out on my own?"

Dammit.

I pushed upward and dusted grass off my jeans to give myself time to think up which lie might fool him. Decided not to be that stupid. We'd been friends long enough he'd notice a lie, especially since he was looking for one.

Better to change the subject.

"There's always something I'm hiding from you." I patted my pockets for the gift. "I'm a man of mystery."

I tugged the gift from the inner pocket of my jacket. "For the wife." I handed him the box, which was roughly the size of my hand.

He took hold of it but didn't draw it toward him, so that we were both holding the box. Or rather, he was holding it to keep me still, to keep me there with him. "You're coming in."

"Of course I'm coming in. It's not a party without me."

"If you think you can bring trouble into my house—"

"—I know, I know. You'll kick my ass." I made to move past him, but he shifted his weight so the bulk of him—and Zayvion was a big man—was in my way.

"No. If you bring trouble into my house, I will handle it. With you. Or without you. But I'd prefer with you."

There was a lot to unpack there. I'd been avoiding him and Allie. I'd been living a life filled with secrets I'd rather he didn't find out. I thought he and Al would be too busy raising their daughter to notice my absence.

But we had grown up together in the magic world. It was foolish of me to think he'd forget that. Forget me.

For his safety, for his daughter's, there were some things better locked up, stowed away, unseen.

"Looking for some excitement? Yeah, I knew it." I released the box, grinned like this was all a big joke. Hey, buddy, buddy. Just mates shooting the shit.

"What I know," Zay went on like I wasn't talking, which: rude, "is that you are hiding something. For some time now.

"What I know is, Terric is in on it. What I know is, it is dangerous. Do you know how I know it's dangerous?"

"Because you're paranoid?"

"Because you are trying to protect me, protect Allie, and protect our daughter."

I gave him a bigger grin. Added a patented eyebrow waggle.

Move along. Nothing to see here. Aren't you over-estimating me? Aren't you giving me way more credit than I'm due?

"That doesn't sound like me, Z. You know I come running at the slightest hint of danger."

Zayvion, who had once been one of the most powerful magic users in Portland, who had the skill and knowledge to be able to use magic to take away people's memories and give them new, false lives—and had done so on several occasions—was a man to fear.

I'd never feared him.

Well, almost never.

But I'd never been dumb enough to underestimate him either.

And from that look in his eye, I had been very, very dumb lately.

"You know I'm the kind of man who can't be half-assed to do anything that doesn't involve," I held up my thumb, "beer. Or two," flew him the finger, "a shitload of money."

Eyebrow twitch again.

"I know exactly what kind of man you are, Shamus," he said.

Well, hell. So much for keeping secrets secret.

When caught dead to rights, I'd always found it

best to admit fully, well, partially, okay, at least the smallest portion of the truth possible.

"It's not a problem," I said. "Old Authority paperwork bureaucracy crap. We've got it handled."

He just gave me a long hard look. "You are so full of shit."

I opened my mouth to...well, agree, because he was not wrong...when the door to the house opened, spilling warm yellow light out into the lavenders of dusk.

"You boys coming in?"

CHAPTER 2

Allie Beckstrom-Jones stood in that doorway, and somehow instead of being cast in shadows, the light found her. She still wore her hair short, just above her shoulders, and had a rocking figure, though it was smoother now, all the hardest edges of pain and sacrifice eased away by a few years of living without the cost of magic.

The years, at least the recent ones, had been good to her. So had having her own little family of three— her, Zay, and little Ramona Jo.

"Al," I nodded. "Want to call your man off? He seems to think I'm gonna start something tonight. Throw down in the backyard. Old bare knuckle brawlin'."

Zay shook his head, but the warning look said volumes.

Allie tensed slightly. She and Zayvion might not be in the middle of each other's minds like back when magic was readily available to everyone on earth, but they were still Soul Complements.

Their souls were tied together in unbreakable ways, with or without magic being part of the binding.

Pretty sure they could still talk mentally to each other.

Which was cool.

And a little creepy.

"Happy birthday, by the way, love," I said.

Stone strolled up next to me, his wings spread, and stepped on my foot.

"Very much, ow, mate."

He growled, ears flicking back.

"Yeah, yeah." I pushed his head and tried to free my foot. "You are very fierce and tackled me to the ground. A-plus gargoyling. And you," I said to Zay, "are in my way. It's like you don't want me to join the party."

"Too late," Allie said, moving aside and snapping her fingers at Stone. "Party's over. Has been for an hour. Nola and Paul just left."

"Oh, well then, I'll just..."

"Get in," Zay and Allie said at the same time.

Allie, at least, smiled. "There's leftover cake," she

said. "You're going to read Ramona her favorite book that I've read a thousand times."

"Do I look like a bedtime story uncle?"

"You look like a bedtime story uncle who wants a beer."

"Bring on the bedtime stories!"

Stone shifted off my foot.

We moved forward together. Me with Stone on one side snuffling like a vacuum cleaner, and Zayvion on the other, big and silent as a shadow.

Flashes of our past, of all the times we had moved together, hunted together, worked magic together, spun out like an endless mural in my mind.

I missed it. Missed us practically living in each other's pockets. Missed fighting the good fight to make the world better, safer.

Death magic stirred in me, and I pushed it away.

Our past was our past. There was no bringing it back now. Too much had changed.

Then I was at the doorway where Allie still waited. The golden light that poured around her pulled away the darkness I seemed unable to escape, and a different world, the world of our now, surrounded me.

"About time," Allie said softly as I drew near. She pulled me into a hug, and I wrapped my arms around her.

It had been awhile, more than that, since I'd seen her.

Death magic wasn't so hungry that I had to fight it to keep it from hurting her. Terric and I had gotten our particular little magical burdens mostly under control.

For the first time in a long time—years—I hugged her back and pecked her cheek. Then I shoved at her as she tried to give me that serious searching expression.

Allie had been a Hound back when magic ruled the streets. She used to make money tracking down magic users who were using magic illegally.

She had a nose and a knack for spotting when things were off, when something wasn't lining up.

She was good at uncovering lies.

I did not want her looking at me any longer than necessary.

"Happy birthday, Al," I said. "Where's my beer?"

She gave me a look that said she was on to me, but relented and stepped into the house, her hand lingering in mine to draw me forward as if she were afraid I'd spook and bolt back out the door.

The house smelled of fresh flowers, a garden of blossoms, and pizza. I didn't know why their house smelled so good, even when there weren't fresh flowers, but no matter the season, Allie and Zayion's home smelled of spring.

"Food first," she said pointing at the pizza boxes on

the table and counter tops. "I have enough pizza left over to feed half of Portland for a week."

"That's what happens when you tell people to bring their favorite dish." I followed her into the living room.

Stone pushed past me, burbling in a high sing-songy tone I'd never heard before.

"Pizza can't be everyone's favorite dish." She dropped down into the loveseat and waved toward the kitchen.

"But everyone brought pizza, didn't they?"

She made a face at me.

I thought about staying there and rubbing it in a little more, but a flurry of noise and motion was headed our way.

"Unc Saym!" The mini-tornado named Ramona Jo tore into the room, Stone trotting happily behind her.

Ramona wore a bright yellow nightgown with tiny green frogs on it.

"Ro-Jo!" I bent and swooped her up into my arms, making her squeal. She was three now, and I was surprised how much heavier she was since the last time I'd been here.

Maybe Zayvion was right. Maybe I'd been gone too long.

"When did you learn to fly?" I asked, settling her in my arms.

"Stone and gumbear I eat and light a pretty. So a pretty!" She hadn't stopped talking since she entered the room.

Her hands, which smelled of strawberries, slapped my cheeks, nose, poked at my mouth and grabbed at my hair. I didn't know if the pat down was because she was hopped up on candy or was trying to make sure I was real.

Whatever she was doing, it was sticky and left me with a poke to the eye.

"Careful, Ro-Jo," I said.

"Carefo," she repeated. Then she babbled about Stone and, if I was piecing this together right, the candy he'd smuggled to her.

"Stone," Allie groaned. "She was in bed."

Stone's eyes went wide, and his ears pricked up. The epitome of innocence.

"No, we've talked about this. When Ramona is in bed, you don't sneak her out."

"Gargoyle pulled off a jailbreak, eh?" I asked. "Clever boy."

"No," Allie said. "Not clever boy. He picks every lock, opens every door, pops every window.

"No matter how many times we tell him bedtime means Ramona stays in bed, we find them in the kitchen under the table, or under a blanket, eating cookies, or playing with toys."

"Playing with toys? Miscreants. I say lock 'em up and throw away the key."

"Not helping, Shame."

"You're a criminal, Stoney," I said. "If you need to hide out from the warden, come on over to my place."

Stone cooed and his wings trembled, happy with that idea.

"Shame." Allie pointed at me to shut it. Then she moved her finger to Stone. "You are not off the hook, mister."

He cooed and looked to the right. Having suddenly discovered his basket of blocks which were always left out for him in the corner, he made a dash for it.

"Stone," Allie said again. "I mean it. No more sneaking her out. No more hiding in closets or the garden shed or the back of the car. No more carrying her up into the attic or the trees. Are you listening to me?"

The gargoyle turned and held up his favorite block, which had a drawing of a block on it. He burbled a question, then placed the block on his head.

He looked like a total dork.

"Being cute won't get you out of this," Allie said.

He quickly grabbed another block and balanced it on his nose. This block had a happy face on it.

"Cute," Allie conceded, "but you're still in trouble.

All right," she made to stand, "let's get everyone back to bed."

"I got it." Zay walked over to me, his arms out.

Ramona had stopped patting my face but had moved on to kicking.

"Easy, monster," I grunted, shifting her heels away from my danger zone.

She squealed.

For a second, I thought I was holding her wrong, but Zayvion plucked her up out of my hands like she weighed nothing and draped her over his shoulder.

"Sack 'tatoes!" she yelled at the floor. "Stone, 'tatoes!"

Stone took that as his call to duty. He bolted across the room and followed behind them, blocks forgotten.

He tipped his head sideways and burbled in her upside-down face, sticking his tongue out. She giggled and shrieked.

The neighbors a mile away heard that.

"Got lungs," I noted.

"Tell me about it." Allie closed her eyes and rubbed at her forehead. She took a deep, slow breath. "It's a lot sometimes."

Zayvion's low voice rumbled out from Ramona's room upstairs, and Allie smiled.

"But you love it," I said.

She nodded, a smile tugging her lips. "I love my life."

She opened her eyes, and they were ocean glass green, light through the first leaves of spring. "I love all the people in my life."

"Aw, look at Mama Beckstrom-Jones. All soft and happy."

That did something I hadn't expected. Her eyebrow twitched and those eyes, which had been spring-dreamy green, turned shell hard.

"All my people in my life, including you, Shame."

"Of course you love me," I said. "I'm very loveable."

She stood, and I could see the frustration all over her, in how she put her hands on her hips, then dropped them, in how she rested her weight on her back foot, then lifted up onto the balls of her feet, in that frown.

"Kitchen." She pointed.

"Bossy. I can get into that. But what would Zayvion say, you wicked thing?"

She pushed on my shoulder to start my march. "He'd say it's about time I did this."

"Did what?"

I stepped into the kitchen. The table was still covered in pizzas, several extra boxes stacked on the counter.

I took a chair in front of the pizza with the most stuff on top and helped myself to a large slice.

"We know you've been dodging us." She opened the fridge, pulled out a bottle of Pirate Stout and handed it to me.

"Why would I dodge you?" I said around a mouthful of delicious.

"We have our ideas. But I'd rather hear it from you."

I popped the cap with my ring and tipped the neck of the beer her way. "You start."

I drank—damn that was good beer—and braced for her and Zay having somehow figured out that Terric and I could still access magic.

Braced for her and Zay to have somehow figured out that magic, which had been locked away for years, had found a way to the surface again and was popping up in hot spots all over Portland.

Hot spots of magic Terric and I were busting our ass to shut down before anyone noticed, or worse, accessed it.

"What are you and Terric doing with magic?"

"Nothing."

"Shame."

"No one can access magic," I said. "We're not accessing magic. Why do you think we're doing something with it? Is something weird happening?"

I leaned forward and put on my concerned face. "Is something going on?"

She narrowed her eyes. "You have never been a very good liar."

I smiled. "How would you know? Maybe I've always been lying to you. Maybe I never have. And also, I'd like to point out, *you* are avoiding answering *me*, love. What trouble are you and Zayvion mixed up in now? Tell Unc Saym."

"I know you, Shame. You're ass-deep in trouble and won't admit it."

I opened my mouth to tell her I had no idea what she was talking about when the back door, the one leading straight into the kitchen, opened, and Terric Conley, the yin to my yang strode into the room.

CHAPTER 3

Terric was taller than me, which was annoying.

He was also a hell of a lot better looking than me.

That was annoying too.

White hair to my black, lean model-like build to my junkyard dog thin, he was also the only other person in the world who could secretly use magic.

Life magic, to be specific. Opposite my Death magic.

Which made sense. We were also Soul Complements, just like Allie and Zay, except unlike Allie and Zay, I was straight, he was gay, and he had a boyfriend.

While we would never be a married couple (thank the mercies) we could read each other in an instant.

"Ter!" I said, then dialed back the desperate cheerfulness. Not quick enough, if Allie rolling her eyes meant anything. "Told you it'd be nothing but pizza for days."

Terric paused in the doorway. It was just a split second, but in it, he read volumes, sorting everything I was mentally shoveling his way.

"Happy birthday, Allie." He moved across the kitchen to deposit a kiss on her cheek and give her a hug.

He looked like a movie star doing it too, the jerk.

He pressed an elegantly wrapped box into her hand then turned toward me. "Shame, you stood me up."

"What was I supposed to do this time?" I chewed, swallowed. "Scoop fungus out of the fridge? I am not cleaning that vegetable drawer. You killed 'em. You gotta bury 'em."

He scowled. "We were going to clean the basement."

Oh shit. That was code for magic going haywire. New hot spot in town? Did someone find it yet?

"Is it flooding again?"

"Yes. You said you'd get the boxes off the floor. I'm not moving all your shit on my own. Do you want mold, Shamus? We don't need mold. Our house has enough problems."

"*My* house," I corrected. "It is my house. You and Dash just moved in and never moved out."

I was on my feet, opening pizza boxes, looking for one that was at least three quarters of a pie, because I figured it was going to be a long night.

Finding the hot spots wasn't always easy, and Dash was out of town. I hoped Terric had already called our friend, Cody Miller. We'd need him to help us track down the hot spot so we could put the damn thing out.

"Al, it's been great." I shoved the box at Terric, then tipped the beer and drank it down. "Good job getting a year older."

Terric glided to the door and held it open, looking unhurried, even though I knew we needed to hustle. The cool wet-leaf and mossy-soil smells of autumn poured into the room.

"Happy birthday," Terric said again. "Sorry we're ducking out like this. Let's make a time when we can all get together soon. Shame? Flood."

"Jesus, Mother. Coming," I grouched.

Terric stepped out. I was right on his heels.

He stopped so abruptly, I ran into his shoulder.

"Fuck, Ter. Warn a guy."

"Both of you," Zayvion, the asshole, had gone around the house to block our exit, "back in the house."

I glanced over my shoulder. Allie's arms were crossed.

"Flooding," I said, "I have books down there. Important books."

"Since when do you read?" Allie asked.

"Rude. I read."

"Porn?" Allie asked.

"Yes. It's my important porn."

"Zay," Terric said, "I am sorry we have to leave, but the basement is literally flooding. We can talk later, okay?"

"No," Zay rumbled. "We talk now."

Terric leaned back just a bit. It might look like he was giving in, but really, he was getting ready to fight. "That can wait."

"We'll help bail out your basement."

"My basement," I said.

"We don't want to bother you," Terric said.

"It's no bother. We're all friends, right?"

"But it's Allie's birthday. I'm not going to let you bail out our basement on her birthday."

They stared at each other for several heartbeats. I wasn't sure who was going to win this one, and I didn't want to have to actually push Zayvion out of the way, but I would.

Magic was trying to break the bars we'd thrown it behind. Time was not on our side.

Then Zay's boots scuffed the stone steps as he moved aside.

Good.

Terric walked past Zay and so did I.

I gave Zayvion a jaunty salute. "Thanks for the pizza. Which I will totally not eat while reading porn."

Zay didn't smile. Didn't laugh. He watched me, those hammered gold eyes hard and suspicious.

They knew we were hiding something, and we were running too damn close to them finding out.

"They know," I said quietly, too quietly for Zay to hear as we made our way to our cars.

"They don't," Terric countered.

"Oh, no. They know."

We paused at Terric's car, him on the driver's side, me on the passenger's. For a moment, I'd forgotten I'd brought my own damn car.

Terric stared past me at Zayvion.

I glanced over my shoulder. Allie was there too, right next to him, both of them bathed in the soft yellow light of the kitchen, disapproval just dripping off of them.

"Did you tell them?" Terric asked.

"Might be stupid, but I'm not suicidal, mate."

"Since when?"

I pressed my fingers to my chest. "Like you don't even know me." I spun and strode to my car.

I didn't show it, and I was pretty sure he didn't notice it, but that was a damn good question he asked. One that shook me.

Since when had I given up on the inevitability that

using Death magic equaled an early, and often horrifying, death?

Maybe I'd given up on it when we locked magic away for a second time.

Or—and this I didn't want to admit—maybe I'd given up on my early demise when Terric had moved into my house, claimed his space in my life, and refused to leave.

Refused to leave me, Death magic and all.

Jesus. When had life gotten, if not good, better?

And why was I still waiting for it all to go to hell?

I paused with my hand on the handle of my car door which was slightly ajar. Strange.

Pretty sure I'd shut the door. Although half a ton of gargoyle had swooped down on me and made a pancake of my spleen.

It was very possible I hadn't shut it hard enough for it to latch completely.

"Getting sloppy, Flynn," I muttered, scanning the sky.

No gargoyle.

Good.

Scanned the yard.

Just two angry Beckstrom-Joneses.

Good enough.

Gave them both a slow parade wave, which earned me the bird from Allie.

Chuckling, I ducked down into my car, started it and took off after Terric who hadn't waited to see if I was following.

Because of course I was.

I figured I always would now.

We were hooked together in a way I didn't think I'd ever be able to escape.

For good or bad.

Oh, let's face it. With my luck, it was gonna be bad all the way down. And I planned to enjoy every damn minute.

CHAPTER 4

Terric led us out of St. John's, over the gothic spired St. John's Bridge that crossed the Willamette River, and toward Forest Park.

He was over the speed limit by ten, so I knew he was trying to get somewhere, but not so fast he'd catch the attention of police.

He guided us down toward the river, across railroad tracks and into the industrial district. Then he drove the narrow road that snaked past old warehouses, factories, and rusted chain-link fences.

He came to a stop in a gravel lot beside a small pump station that had seen better days.

I pulled up next to him, killed the engine, and got out into the cold evening air.

It was dark enough here, and untraveled enough, drifters used it on the regular.

They'd left evidence: a burned-out campfire, discarded beer cans, the remnants of a canvas painting —frame smashed and broken—and fast food wrappers cobwebbing the old tangled blackberry bushes.

Terric got out of his car and pointed north. "This way."

He didn't have to tell me. I could feel it.

Magic boiled right beneath the surface, rich and hot and absolutely begging to be set free.

We didn't know why magic was sparking like this, hot spots popping up in Portland's random out-of-the-way places. But so far, we'd been able to put out the random embers before they turned into a full-blown magic eruption.

He stopped and knelt where the gravel met old, dry summer weeds.

I patted my pocket for a cig, lit up, and blew smoke before crouching next to him.

"Ashes again." Terric touched the soft gray feather remains of whatever had been burned here.

He rubbed his fingers. "Is the magic burning something, or is someone burning something else to trigger the magic?"

"If we knew, mate, maybe we wouldn't be out chasing our own asses in the middle of the night."

"It's ten o'clock, Shame."

"So?"

"It's not the middle of the night."

"It's cutting into my gaming time, and that means it's piss-me-off-o'clock."

"I don't think magic is doing this." Terric pressed his palm to the dirt and gravel. "It's not even warm."

"Magic doesn't have to heat to burn." I sucked on the cig, held the inhale and touched the same patch of ground.

Magic licked at my palm, maybe recognizing that I was one of the people who had locked it away for good.

Maybe testing to see if I was the key to set it free.

Terric was right. It didn't feel like magic had leaked through its containment enough to actually burn something down to ash.

Which left us with the only other theory. Someone was trying to break magic free.

"Dash find anything new in the books?" I asked, my words carrying the exhale of smoke into the darkness.

"Nothing that says: Step one: burn this to wake up magic." He dusted fingers on his knee. "We'll keep looking. It's a lot of books to get through."

He stood, tucked his thumbs into his front pockets, then did a slow circle.

"No one's here, mate," I said.

"I know. It's just...it feels like we're being watched."

"Couple old guys like us? Who would be watching?"

"Old?"

"You're what, forty? Fifty?"

"Thirties. I'm in my thirties and you know that."

"Still older than me."

"Obviously, because you act like a child."

"And you act like a grumpy old man."

"Only when you're around."

"Which is all the damn time. You sure you and Dash don't want a bigger place? Somewhere far, far away from me? Like Canada?"

"Canada is only one state away from here, and we're not moving. Someone's watching."

I grunted and pushed up, ignoring Terric's smirk at the noise my knees made as I got up out of a crouch. "Where?"

He frowned, did the slow circle again. "I don't know."

"Dangerous?"

"Doesn't feel hostile."

I might give him shit, but I trusted his instinct.

"Worth tapping the source and throwing Illusion?"

He held his breath, then exhaled. "No, I think we

can lock this hot spot down, have a beer, make it all look like an innocent drug deal, and move on."

"Innocent drug deal. Ah, Conley. Man after my wretched old heart."

"Thought you were young."

"I am. But this heart has seen some shit."

"When are you going to start dating again?"

"Did I black out?" I asked. "I saw your mouth moving but no sound came out."

He glared at me, and I glared right back. My love life, and lack of it, was none of his business.

"You're dealing," he finally said.

"Drugs? Of course I'm dealing," I said. "You better have brought the beer."

"In the car. It's the crap stuff, though. Allie had Pirate Stout," he complained.

"My how the angels have fallen. Crap beer. A fake drug deal." I grinned. "Sure you don't want to move out before you start hanging out at dive bars and waking up in strange beds?"

He stuck his hands on his hips, utterly exasperated, but there was a smile tugging on that scowl.

My phone buzzed. I ignored it. Whoever it was, could wait.

Magic, however, could not.

I took a final drag of the cig, pinched it between my

fingers, and let it drop, grinding it out with my boot heel.

Terric's phone rang, some sort of orchestral movement, then mine buzzed again.

"Dash?" I asked.

He had already pulled his phone out of his jacket because he was responsible like that. "Allie."

"Yeah, don't answer it yet, mate. We can take our punishment after we cork this magic leak."

He wanted to argue. To say, "what if it's important?" But he silenced the tone and tucked the device back into his pocket.

I just let mine buzz all it wanted.

"Might not be Allie," he said of my phone.

"Won't find out until we're done." I waved toward the burned ground.

Terric drew a slim black leather case out of his breast pocket, something that could hold a couple slim cigars, or perhaps fancy pens.

He opened it and handed me a glossy black pen—yes, very fancy—the barrel hand-turned and made of a mix of material and acrylic that he and I had added a lot of magical influences to, including chanting, rare metals, and our own blood.

He took the other pen, white as moonlight, made from the same sort of magical items.

Death. Life.

Back when magic flowed freely, all one had to do was memorize the glyphs that magic flowed through and then, with intent and the correct drawing of that glyph in the air, magic would snap to and get it done.

Now the only way to get to magic was through old, outdated primal tokens and practices. Things that were more than a little unreliable, half bullshit, half brilliance.

Things like herbs.

Like chanting.

Like using ink infused with a little of our own blood to draw very old symbols into the earth. Symbols that were halves of different spells, guiding magic to twist and turn back in on itself.

To convince it to sink back down and go back to sleep again.

We uncapped the pens. He took north, the guiding position, several feet away from me. I took the south.

He knelt, and I crouched, and we pressed nibs to dirt, gravel, and concrete, and began scratching and sketching.

The symbols were familiar but bastardized almost beyond recognition.

We drew Hold and Freeze and Sleep. We drew Beneath and Burrow, and most of all Contain, creating new channels for the river of magic to flow through, creating a loop to send the magic back, deep, deep down into the earth where it belonged.

This kind of magic was still trial and error. Dash and Cody had helped us do the heavy lifting to research which odd sorts of old hoodoo worked on the hot spots.

Terric and I did the dirty work of bullying magic back to where it belonged.

We circled counter clockwise as we drew. Terric added chanting to the mix, because he was old school Faith magic and had always added chanting to the mix.

I just tried to keep the lines of the bastardized glyphs clean and clear, and wished I had another cigarette.

That "someone's watching us" thing had me on edge.

Why had Allie called? Was there trouble? Was she just wanting to yell at us?

We had almost reached opposite points of the circle, Terric a degree away from south and me a few inches from north when something flashed at the corner of my eye.

It was fire, neon white and blue, a flash of paper burning, of chemicals flaming purple, green.

Magic surged from the circle we hadn't closed, and lashed out. I slashed the last symbol into the dirt, shifting the half-finished spell, forcing Contain to twist into Block. I pivoted on the balls of my feet, hand tracing the glyph for Shield in the air and pulled on the Death magic inside me to fuel it.

As if magic worked the way it used to work.

As if it would shield me, shield Terric.

As if magic would listen to any of us anymore.

Magic had always been fast, fast enough it was hard to see with the naked eye.

But everything around me slowed.

It was easy now to see magic—that costly, dangerous, beautiful god-maker force—sparking like fire gulping oxygen.

Magic that was not contained deep in the earth or in the spells we had cast. Magic that had broken free.

It leaped out of the ground and caught fire in the trash-covered bushes, the center of it blindingly bright.

This wasn't just magic rising up out of the earth.

This wasn't just magic jumping free of its bonds and randomly striking fire.

This magic was focused, hungry, determined to devour something in that bush.

Paper? No. There was color there, paint.

There was canvas. The painting.

Magic was devouring the broken painting.

Points to me for noticing the source of the problem.

Points to magic for not waiting for me to step up to the pitch before taking aim and firing.

Too slow. That one thought filled my brain.

Too slow to stop magic, too slow to dodge, too slow to jump in front and save Terric from the hit.

Magic whip-cracked, searing through the air like a neon white arrow, aiming straight for our heads.

Fuck. Me.

CHAPTER 5

A wall of gray, broad, fast, filled my vision.

Time ticked, speeding up all at once, then snapping into place.

Stone. The wall of gray was Stone.

Magic hit him, and he absorbed it, then he attacked the painting.

He shoveled it out from under the bush with his claws, digging, tearing, snarling. He howled and shook it like he could break its neck.

The sound was so primal it made the hair stand up on the back of my neck.

I took a step back.

Terric was next to me, hands raised in the stance I recognized for Block.

Stone growled and wadded up the painting,

smashing and pounding the fire and canvas until it was a compact ball of magic and paint.

Then he opened his huge mouth, rows and rows of sharp teeth reflecting the light. He stuck out his long tongue.

And ate the painting.

Stone chewed like the painting was made of spikes, chomping and snarling.

"What in the bloody hell?" I shouted.

"Where the fuck did he come from?" Terric asked.

"What the fuck did you do?" I asked Stone.

Stone just growled louder and kept on chewing.

"You brought him here?" Terric asked.

"The fuck I did." I turned and froze. "Oh, no. Oh, no, no, no."

I shoved the magic pen in my teeth, so I had both my hands free, and ran to my car.

Ramona, still in her yellow nightgown, stood barefoot next to my car.

I bent and scooped her up.

"Ro-Jo." I spit out the pen, not caring where it fell. "What are you doing here, sweetheart?"

My hands were shaking, my voice was shaking. Ramona's fingers were all over my face, and they were cold, her cheeks pink from the night air.

"Baby girl. Sweetheart. What are you doing here?

Where is your mamma? Holy shit, where's your daddy? How did you get here?"

"Unc Saym! I want light. My hand. Unc Saym."

I pulled her to my chest, pressing my hand over her back.

All the horrifying possibilities of her being hurt, lost, frozen to death, killed, slammed through my brain.

"Holy shit, holy shit." I breathed into her hair and shook, holding onto her like she was the last and only precious thing in this world that I'd almost lost.

It took a long time for fear to ebb enough I could hear again.

Ramona was babbling, still patting my face, leaning back in my arms, wanting me to put her down.

My phone vibrated in my pocket. Terric was talking. Calm, soothing tones.

At first, I thought he was trying to keep me calm.

I turned. He was on his phone right beside me, talking to Zayvion.

"We've got her, she's fine. Not a scratch. Yes, Stone too. Shame's car. Yes. We can—" Terric frowned. "It would be better if we just brought them...yes. Yes, but we can...no. Yes, we'll wait."

He stabbed his phone and clenched his fist around it like he was about to huck it into the brush. He jammed it in his pocket.

"Allie and Zay are on their way," he said. "What

the hell were you thinking? Of all the idiotic things to do. Bringing her out here?"

"I didn't bring her here," I yelled.

Ramona shrieked and slapped her hands over her ears, and I bounced her in my arms.

"She must have been in my car," I said at normal volume. "Stone must have snuck her into the back seat."

"You didn't look in the backseat before you got in the vehicle?"

"One: no. Two: fuck you."

"Down down!" Ramona shouted and squirmed, but there was no way I was setting her down. "My light. Mine!"

"No, baby," I said. "No down. No light. You don't have shoes on. The rocks will hurt your feet."

"Down!" she demanded.

"Not gonna work. You are not the first strong woman I've had to say no to."

Ramona pushed on my shoulders, and when that didn't work, she started crying. Loudly.

"Jesus Christ, Shame," Terric said, "you have the paternal instincts of a quokka. Give her to me."

"Quokkas are good parents," I argued.

He reached for her, but I wasn't going to let her out of my arms.

"They throw their babies at predators," he said.

"That's an internet meme."

"That doesn't matter. Give her here."

"Back off." I twisted. "Go deal with the gargoyle."

"Stone!" Ramona wailed, reaching for her buddy.

"Shame," Terric scolded.

"I've got her." I twisted again, planning to take her back to the car.

But Terric was being a dumbass and reached for her just as she kicked me in the nads.

It was enough of a hit that I loosened my hold and bent, giving the little demon her chance to slide out of my arms.

I groaned and tried not to puke.

Ramona ran to Stone, who was smacking his lips and making exaggerated gulping sounds.

"Ramona," Terric called as he darted after her.

I sucked a couple hard breaths and spit. Fuck.

"Wait," I wheezed.

Stone was only a few yards away. Terric had long legs. I would have put good money on him reaching Ramona before she reached Stone.

I would have lost.

Ramona flew across the dirt and gravel, a wisp in the night, her only mission to reach her friend.

"Wait," I called again, staggering forward.

There was no chance in hell I could catch her before Terric.

Stone saw Ramona running at him, her arms out, seeking rescue.

And that massive, magical beast went into protect mode.

He launched to her, his wings pumping to add speed to his spring, and was on her in a split second. He landed beside her, wings spread, big head down, snarling at Terric.

Snarling at me.

"Whoa, buddy," I started.

But Stone did not whoa. He bared his teeth.

For all that Stone was a total dingus of a puppy, when he was in protect mode, he was very dangerous, very deadly, and would tear a mountain down to save the people he loved.

Stone and I were friends.

But he loved Ramona Jo.

Terric slowed, then stopped altogether. He held up his hands. "It's okay, Stone. We're trying to help her. She's cold and doesn't have shoes."

The gargoyle's ears flicked up, then back again. He growled.

"Ya' big dope," I said, "we're on your side."

Ramona was still crying, though it sounded fake now. She threw herself into him, her arms looping around his wide neck.

And Stone absolutely lit up with magic.

He was still Stone, the gargoyle who had been brought to life by magic, and remained alive because Cody Miller liked him and wanted him to stay alive.

When Cody had done his part in healing magic, Stone was the one rare magical creature that remained.

But now every line of Stone was painted in neon. The same wild colors that had burned in the painting were now alive and burning through him.

Where Ramona touched him, the magic glowed brighter.

"Do you see that?" Terric exhaled.

The crunch of tires traveling at speed broke the quiet of the night.

"Lube up," I said. "We are about to be fucked."

Headlights swung over the road in a wild curve. The car skidded to a stop, both doors opening almost before the car stopped rocking.

Allie and Zayvion were storm and lightning.

Back when they could sling magic, if I'd seen them headed my way with those looks on their faces, I would have drawn Shield and run like hell.

They ran at us, and I wasn't dumb enough to stand between them and their daughter.

"Ramona," Allie called out.

Ramona looked over her shoulder, then turned in the shelter of Stone's wings. She was sniffing and babbling about light and Stone.

Then she said, "Mine," and pressed her palm on the neon-lit curve of his cheek.

The neon light, the magic Stone had chewed and swallowed, rushed to that contact point, and poured into her hand.

Allie scooped Ramona up, but it was too late.

Ramona's arm swirled with beautiful vines of magic, soft blues and pinks and yellows against her darker skin. Her eyes flashed with the same soft light and then...

...then nothing.

The magic was gone. The little girl was just a little girl again, the gargoyle once more just a gargoyle.

Zayvion wrapped Allie and Ramona in his arms, and they stood that way for a moment.

Then Allie spun to face me, absolute fury masking her features. "Jesus, Shame."

I threw up my hands. "I didn't know she was in the car. I didn't kidnap her. You know I'd never do that. I'd never hurt her."

She wanted to tell me off, wanted a target for that anger and fear. Instead, she pulled Ramona closer to her.

"Ramona, this is not okay. You can not leave the house without mommy or daddy. This was dangerous. You were not safe."

"Light. Light, Mama."

"I know, I saw. But Stone should have stayed at home too." She turned to the gargoyle. "No more. No more leaving the house without us knowing, Stone. Never again."

Stone rumbled and dipped his head, his ears flat, every line of him droopy with guilt.

"What did you do to Stone?" Zay paced behind Allie and around the spellwork we hadn't finished.

Spellwork we shouldn't have been doing. Spellwork that shouldn't even work.

He glanced down, then back up, his gaze holding Terric's. "What did you two do here?"

"I didn't know Ramona snuck out, Zayvion."

Zay moved in on Terric.

It wasn't a threat. It didn't have to be. Some things were understood between friends, and Terric and Zay had been friends for years.

"What are you doing with magic?" He pointed down at the sketching.

"It's old stuff. Outdated ideas about magic. Shame and I just—"

"No," Zay cut him off. "Don't lie. We know. We know you and Shame have been doing something for a long time now. Something you don't want us to know."

"And you just assume it's magic?"

Zay held Terric's gaze a moment longer, but Terric

was glaring back at him, his mouth pressed in an angry line.

Zay turned his scowl on me. "I'm not an idiot. Don't treat me like one. Stone was filled with magic, visible magic. My daughter touched it.

"I want an explanation. I want the truth. Or we are going to find ourselves on the opposite sides of a very bad situation."

"What are you going to do," I taunted, "call the cops on us? Call the Head of the Authority on us? Oh, wait, the Authority doesn't exist anymore."

His hand was fast, but so was I.

I ducked and blocked, my fist meeting his wrist. I thought he was going for my head, but instead, he grabbed my jacket and held up the pen I'd dropped.

I punched him in the ribs just because I could, and received a satisfying grunt.

"What bullshit is this?" Zay held the pen out of my reach because he was tall and also because he was an ass.

"It's just a pen," Terric said. "We were experimenting with old magical practices. That's all, Zayvion."

Zay uncapped the pen, brought the nib to his mouth, and touched it with the tip of his tongue.

"Blood magic." He spit and recapped the pen. He let go of my jacket, shoving me back.

Then he pointed at the ground again. "Talk. Or yes, Shame, I will call the police, who haven't forgotten what magic can do in the wrong hands. They are more than willing to lock up anyone who can still access it."

"We can't access—" Terric started.

"No." Zay's hand slashed downward. "You've broken every damn rule and lock we put on it. For what?"

"We didn't—" I said.

"The hell you didn't. You have involved my daughter in this. Magic, Shamus? What the fuck did you think was going to happen?"

"I thought my best friend was going to go on living his happy life with his happy family and stay the hell out of my business!" I yelled. "Like that's too damn fucking much to ask."

I figured another punch was headed my way, but he shook his head and took a deep breath, rolling his shoulders back.

"You *are* my family," he said. "You ass."

"Dadda, light?" Ramona asked. "Light?"

"We know magic has been...shifting," Zay said, as Allie hushed Ramona. "We can feel it. Just tell us: What have you done? What are you doing? And what are we going to do to help with that?"

"You don't need to be part of this," Terric said calmly. "Magic is still locked up. You can tell.

Everyone can tell. We haven't changed anything. We don't need your help."

Technically true.

But we had kept Life magic and Death magic for ourselves. I carried Death magic in my body, and Terric carried Life magic. That made us the de facto caretakers of magic. We kept the city safe. We paid the price magic demanded.

That price wasn't pain, like the old days. It was a battle for control over the magic we carried. Go too long without killing something and the Death magic in my bones would lash out and devour everything within a mile radius.

I killed to feed it and keep it under control. Sometimes those kills were small—bugs, plants, random wood planks. Sometimes those kills were large: like the magic criminals on our ex-teacher Victor's hit list.

Terric managed Life magic via regular visits to hospitals, and on one icy, endless night last winter, responding to car accidents and ambulance calls.

Yes, we could use magic, but every time we did, it tried to slip free of our control.

"Dadda!" Ramona yelled. "My light!"

Light bloomed bright and strong. I thought another car had turned our way, headlights on high.

Or maybe a truck, or cops with a spotlight.

But the air tasted of cherry blossoms and cotton

candy, and I knew the light that filled the air was not mechanical.

It was magical.

From Zayvion's stunned expression, Terric's whispered curse, and Allie's gasp, they all knew it too.

Stone just cooed happily.

Because my goddaughter, little Ramona Jo Beckstrom-Jones, was in her mother's arms, holding her hand out like she expected someone to give her candy.

And from that chubby little hand poured magic.

A lot of magic.

Bright magic.

Light.

It was a very simple spell. One of the first a magic user learned. It was also impossible.

"Well, fuck me," I said.

CHAPTER 6

I do not invite people into my house. My house is my own private hole in which to disappear, get blackout drunk, maybe listen to old prog rock.

I liked being alone. Preferred it.

My house was the perfect escape.

Before Terric and Dash decided they had to move in.

I hadn't found a way to kick them out, so I'd set some rules. The main rule was: Don't invite people over.

Since we'd found a stash of rare magical books and stored them all in my basement, it was a rule they were happy to follow.

We didn't want anyone knowing we still had control over Life magic and Death magic. We didn't want anyone knowing we had other ways to access magic that might be outdated and unrefined, but which still worked just fine, thank you.

Our secret stash of secret books was known to only five people: Me, Terric, Dash, Terric's sister, who had been there when we found them, and Cody Miller.

Cody was the thread that had sewed up magic the last time, healing it so it could be locked away.

Terric's sister was still in college and had transferred to Berkeley. Cody was here in Portland, living the life of an up-and-coming art phenom.

But now there were three people and a gargoyle in my house with me and Terric.

"Coffee?" I offered. "Booze? This feels like a booze moment."

Allie walked straight to the bathroom, Ramona sleeping in her arms. The little girl had fallen asleep hard and fast after using magic. So far, there didn't seem to be any other price she was paying for it.

"Coffee," Allie said. "I'll make it."

"I know how to brew coffee."

She muttered something about cigarettes, dirt, and tar, which I ignored. Then I heard the bath water run, and Allie's patient tone as she washed Ramona.

Ramona was fine, well, uninjured from normal things like running on gravel and being out at night.

I figured Allie's real worry was coming from her daughter absorbing magic and then wielding it.

Yeah, I was a little freaked out about that too.

Terric and Zayvion staked out opposite sides of the living room, arms crossed, scowling at each other.

Ridiculous.

"Sit. Both of you. I'm making coffee, and by coffee, I mean downing a bottle of tequila."

They didn't move. I knew Terric would break first. We'd been caught and there was no talking or glaring our way out of this.

The jig was up.

"I'll help," Terric offered.

"No, you sit. Make him sit too. You're both giving me a rash."

"Just coffee, Shame." Terric looked my way, as if expecting me to be glugging down a fifth already.

I shook my head at him.

He sighed and uncrossed his arms. "Fine. Sit," he said to Zayvion. "Unless I can talk you out of being here?"

Zay walked to the couch and sat, his arm across the back of it. "Nope."

I left them to it and made myself useful pouring water into the pot and scooping out grounds. With that going, I walked out into the cooler air and sat on the back step.

I lit a cigarette, inhaled, and exhaled smoke.

"I know you're there, mate," I said to a man hiding

in the shadow of the overgrown hedge that Terric insisted was my responsibility to keep trimmed.

"My advice? Turn around and skip the clown show while you can."

Cody Miller walked out of the shadows and lifted his hand in a short wave.

He was maybe a year older than me, tanned, yellow hair. He wore a dark turtleneck under a plaid cardigan, a striped vest over that, and a tweed overcoat.

His pants were rolled at the cuff, and while it should look like he'd just fallen out of a thrift store bin, he looked fashionable as hell.

"I was just coming by to see Stone." His stride was a little shortened by the large painting he was lugging in one hand.

"No, you weren't."

"Yeah, no, I wasn't."

He propped the canvas against a spindly rosebush and leaned on the stair railing next to me. "You found the hot spot?" he asked.

"Yes."

"They followed you?"

"Ramona and her dumb gargoyle followed us. Al and Z followed them."

"What are you telling them?"

"The truth."

Cody just stood there staring at the house and breathed for a moment.

His mind had been broken for many years. Now he had this thing about him that made you think he saw more than the outside of people.

That he saw all the magic hidden in the world, and just as easily, all the soul hidden in a person.

"All of the truth?" he asked.

"Only as much as we have to." I blew a thin stream of smoke. "Why are you here? Afraid we'll rat you out?"

"I'm not hiding anything." He stuffed his hands in his pockets. "Or I didn't think I was, but I might be wrong."

"Do I want an explanation? This night has been ass."

"I think I know what's causing the hot spots."

I finished my cigarette and flicked it into the damp moss. "Welcome to the clown show, mate," I said. "Coffee's burning."

He clomped up the stairs after me into the house, bringing the painting with him.

Allie was in the kitchen, pouring coffee into four cups.

"Hi, Allie," Cody said.

She took a look at him, at the painting, then pulled another cup out of the cupboard. "Cream and sugar?"

"Yes, please," he said. "I'll, um, just take this in...there?" He pointed toward the living room.

"Go," I said. "I'll help bring coffee out."

He left the kitchen, and I picked up two of the mugs. "Ramona okay?"

Allie tucked her hair behind her ears, and I could tell she was still angry and afraid of what could have happened to her daughter.

"Not a scratch or bruise on her," she said, pushing her emotions aside. "I asked her to use magic again. To use Light and she says she can't do it.

"Then she started talking about Stone and magic, which she thinks is light. I put her to sleep in your bed."

"Hope you didn't let Stone in there with her."

"He's in the living room, sulking."

"Allie, I'm sorry. If I'd taken a minute and looked in the back seat..."

"No, it's okay. I wasn't mad at you."

At my look, she gave me a wry smile. "I wasn't *only* mad at you. I was angry they'd snuck out, angry it took me minutes to realize she wasn't in her bed.

"She wasn't in her bed, Shame. And you fucking didn't answer the phone." She slapped my shoulder and tears glittered at the bottom of her eyes.

"Al, there is nothing in this world that can hurt her as long as Stone is with her. You know he'll always look after her. You know how protective he is."

"That doesn't make it better. I knew he would protect her. But she got out. She could have been taken, lost. My heart just stopped. I didn't know what to do."

"You did," I said. "You called us. And you were right. She was with us. Good instinct, mama bear."

"That was all Zay. He knew they must have snuck into your or Terric's car. He was the first to call, the first to act. I just stood there."

"Well, I'm disappointed in you, young lady," I said.

She blinked and slapped my arm again. "Thin line."

"So disappointed. I mean the first time your daughter disappears from out of her bed, you panicked? You froze? Like a normal person? Like half of everyone else in the world? I guess you are just human." I *tsk*ed. "And here I thought you were superhuman."

"Not helping." But the tears were gone and the annoyance was back, so: win. "Why did you get Cody mixed up in this?"

She walked past me into the living room.

"Not everything that goes wrong is my fault, you know." I walked into the room.

All three men were staring at me. "What?" I said. "It's true. Not everything is my fault."

Terric took his coffee from Allie. "Most," he said. "Most of it is."

"You wanna speak up, Conley?"

"Oh, I've been saying it since the day I met you."

"That I'm so much better than you? Smarter, stronger, more handsome. Why, yes. I am the full meal deal."

"You're full of shit, is what you're full of," he muttered.

I handed Cody a cup so I could flip Terric off with both fingers.

"Talk." Zay shifted to make room for Allie beside him.

She leaned back into the crook of his arm, the lines of her fitting perfectly with the bulk of him.

"Yeah, Terric," I said, "talk."

I dropped into the wooden chair next to Stone, who was moping on the rug. I rocked the chair back on two legs until it leaned against the wall.

"Over the last couple months, magical hot spots have been cropping up around town. Shame and I have found a way to force magic back. To shut it down."

"You're using magic." Allie held Terric's gaze, daring him to lie.

"Yes, but not how you are thinking."

"Explain," Zayvion said.

Terric tensed, but I knew the moment when he had run though all of his options and landed on the distasteful one: the truth.

"We found a few documents. Old books." He lifted his fingers like they were nothing, inconsequential.

"Magic books," Allie said. "Where did you find them?"

"It was a private collection. What matters is that we have had them for a while."

I liked how he left out that we'd gotten them off a dead guy who had used magic in ways the books described.

I liked how he didn't mention that that magic use had killed the guy.

She frowned. "That's what you were doing tonight? Dealing with a hot spot?"

"Yes. It's why I came for Shame. Magic is easier to shove back into its box when one person slams the door and the other turns the key."

"Plus, you're Soul Complements," Cody added. "That's a big part of it too."

He wasn't wrong.

"The Blood magic pen?" Zay asked.

"It's not Blood magic—or it's not Blood magic how we used to use it," Terric said. "There are...herbs involved."

Zay's eyebrows lifted, but he rolled his fingers in a keep-going motion.

"Herbs, chanting, drawing on or into specific materials with specific materials. Old stuff. Hoodoo stuff, witch stuff, druid stuff, all of that works now. Or works sometimes," he said.

"Don't get me started on the amount of bull crap information there is in the books. But there are kernels of truth. There are good practices mixed in with all the other fears, superstitions, and poor translations."

"You weren't going to tell us?" Allie asked, but before we could answer, she went on. "Of course you weren't. You do know if you two found a stash of secret books, other people around the world have probably found books too? It's not like Portland is the only place where magic or books exist."

"We know," Cody said.

"We?" She asked icily. "How are you involved in this Cody?"

He shrugged in his best "shucks-ma'am," manner which I knew was sincere.

Allie liked him. He liked her too.

She'd saved his life, he'd saved hers—really all of our lives—when he'd stood as the vessel for dark and light magic to flow into.

When he'd held all the magic in the world in his body and soul and forced it to heal.

"I know when it's happening," he said.

"In the whole world? All the hot spots?" she asked.

"Yes, but you're wrong. It's not happening in all the world. It's only happening here. In Portland."

She inhaled and exhaled. "Okay. That's something. You're sure, though? You can feel it when it happens?"

"Allie," he said softly. "I'm not lying."

"I know. I just... Okay, so how can you tell there's a hot spot?"

He shrugged. "I just can."

"Did you know about the one tonight?" Zay asked.

"Yes. I told Terric. He and Shame...they're better at the dirty work. I'm better at the brain work."

"The hell you are," I laughed.

"You knew where it was going to appear?" Zay, as always, remained focused on the goal at hand.

"Approximately."

"How approximately?"

"Within a few yards."

Allie shook her head. "How? No, I know. You held magic. You carried it. You *were* it. You can feel it.

"I believe you. So, are you the one who told them which spells or rituals or herbs or whatever would work on magic?"

"Some. They have decent instincts."

"I can not believe you," she glared at each of us in

turn, "kept this from us. Don't you trust us? Don't you think we would have your back?

"Haven't we always faced magic and the backlash from it together?" She tucked her hair behind her ear and scowled over her coffee cup. "Haven't we always done the dirty work together?"

Her voice resonated with emotions from the bonds of time we had shared. The bonds of war.

I wasn't someone who had enough of a moral center to feel guilt, but that didn't mean I felt pleased with myself at the moment.

"We were thinking of you," Terric said. "You and Zayvion and your daughter. You all just got out of the dangers that living a life with magic demands. You've just begun to live your lives in a more normal way."

He blew out a breath. "We wanted that for you. We still want that for you."

"It's not your job to decide what our lives are," Allie said. "Maybe we don't want normal. Maybe we're tired of it. Maybe we're a little...bored with normal."

The look on Zay's face was priceless.

"Uh-oh," I said. "Trouble in paradise?"

Zayvion shifted so he could better see her.

She shifted too. Her cheeks were pink. She might have been a little surprised at what she'd just revealed, but she was not taking it back.

"I love our life," she said. "I love our family. I love

our home and I love you. But magic? Left up to these three? Come on."

"Oh, for fuck's sake," I muttered.

He studied her for a moment, then without breaking his very blank expression, said, "Terric's occasionally level-headed."

"Occasionally?" Terric squawked.

Zay sniffed.

"Since when haven't I been level-headed?"

"You did make the mistake of moving in with Shame."

I slurped coffee, enjoying the show. It wasn't often Zay wound Terric up.

"I thought it through very carefully," Terric defended. "That wasn't a mistake."

I straightened in the chair and tipped my chin up.

"It was a massively annoying necessity," Terric said. "I mean, have you seen the man?" He waved vaguely in my direction.

"Out," I growled. "Hell, I'll pay for movers if you'll just let me live in peace."

"Where are the books?" Allie asked.

Zay and Terric were exchanging a look I didn't care for. They looked pleased.

"Annoying?" Zayvion asked him.

"Massively," Terric agreed.

"Oh, to hell with you both. Allie, this way."

Terric's emotions spiked. He was startled I was about to reveal our secret library.

"In for a penny," I said.

He nodded. We were truly and fully busted.

Unless we wanted to figure out a way to Close people with magic and take their memories away, like the old days, Zayvion and Allie were officially in on our secret.

CHAPTER 7

Cody waved us to go. "I'll make sure Stone doesn't get into trouble." He sat on the floor, legs in lotus position and tapped his knee.

Stone flipped over to lie on his back, his head in Cody's lap so Cody could scratch his belly.

I headed down to the basement, Allie following, Terric behind her, and Zay bringing up the rear.

"This is it." I waved my hands at the room as we hit the bottom of the stairs.

Allie took in the shelves Terric and Dash had installed, and the books and totes carefully stacked upon them.

"This is a lot of books, Shame. A library," she said.

"Yeah."

"When you said you found some books, I thought you meant a dozen. At the most."

I just made a what-can-I-say sound.

She turned, hands on hips. "How long have you been hunting this stuff down? How many people have you killed?"

"Two very different questions, and you are getting all worked up over nothing. Okay, from that look, I'll revise my statement. You are getting worked up over the wrong things."

"All the books were in one place, Allie," Terric said.

Zay was already running his fingertip over the spines of the volumes, maybe seeing if he could feel magic in them.

He shouldn't feel anything. The books themselves didn't have magic, but some were very old and contained very accurate information.

"Shame didn't kill anyone for us to get these," Terric said.

"See?" I wagged my finger at her. "Jumping to conclusions. Accusations without evidence. Sloppy detective work, Beckstrom-Jones."

She had already tuned me out. She opened a tote, removed several books, and stacked them carefully on the open spot on the shelf.

"These are...I haven't heard of any of them. Is this a cookbook?" She held it toward Zayvion and Terric, who both glanced at it and replied at the same time. "Yes and no."

Terric threw me a look, reminding me that he and Zay were smarter than me. I flipped him the book-smarts-aren't-everything bird.

"An original Zytershest?" Zayvion's voice held a note of reverence I'd rarely heard. "Terric, is this an original?"

Terric offered Zay a pair of cotton gloves. "I think it is, but it's not like I'm taking these out to be appraised."

Zay slipped the gloves on and carefully removed the book from the glass case Terric and Dash had made such a big fuss about.

"These look like recipes," Allie said. "But they're very specific about what order the ingredients are mixed, and the herbs are...a lot. Silphium? Isn't that extinct?"

"Lots of cultures hid spells and magic in poetry," Terric said.

"Now you did it," I groaned. "He's in teacher mode."

He flicked me a look. "In songs and in recipes," he continued. "The ritual makes it easier to memorize and keeps it out of the hands of people who don't know what they're doing."

I made snoring sounds, but Zayvion grunted in agreement.

Allie shook her head slightly, turning the pages of the recipe book more slowly and carefully.

"These need to be somewhere safe," Zay said.

"Excuse you?" I asked.

He didn't even glance up. "Safer."

"That's not happening," Terric said. "Locking them away in a vault will just draw attention from people whose attention we really don't want."

"Like who?" Zay asked.

"Like whichever part of the Authority that should have been disbanded might still be banded," I said. "Whichever part of the Authority that might be looking for big, obvious signs of people trying to break magic back open. Tap it in unique ways."

I didn't know if there were such people.

But once a secret society of magic users, always a secret society of magic users.

"Have you seen evidence of that kind of thing?" Both Zay and Allie were watching me closely.

From the intensity of their expressions—concern, maybe anger—they were worried about the Authority still monitoring ex-magic users too.

My shoulders relaxed. "Not of the Authority. Or not yet."

"But you think there are people still watching the people who were powerful magic users?" Allie asked.

"I think people don't just walk away from the

ability to use magic, dust their hands, and say it's no big deal."

"We walked away from ever using magic again," she pointed out.

I tipped my head. "Did you? You're here, holding books that are pretty good at tapping at least a little magic."

Her cheeks slashed pink. "Point taken."

"How did you know which spell or process works?" Zay asked.

Terric and I both took a short breath. "So, there's a little more you don't know," Terric said.

Zayvion closed the book and replaced it in the glass case. "Explain."

"Shame and I held onto magic a little longer than most."

The heartbeats of silence were endless.

"Do you still have magic?" Zay finally asked.

Terric shifted his weight and tucked his hand into his pocket. "Not like we did."

"But?" Allie asked.

"But we can reach it. Easier than most."

"With the books?" she pressed.

"And without." He nodded toward the shelves. "But we have to be in contact with someone or something. We can't pull it out of the air like we used to. It takes physical interaction, like writing, touching, contact. We can draw it into spells and cast, especially with the right items."

He paused to consider. "Not like before, but not nothing."

Zayvion rubbed his hand over his mouth and nodded. "We thought so."

That was a calm response to us telling him that we were breaking the rules of the entire world just to scratch our own abracadabras.

"You *thought* so?" I asked. "That's it? You thought so?"

Allie shrugged. "We've known both of you for a long time."

"No," I said. "That's not it. That's not all of it. What aren't you telling *us*?"

"This isn't about us," Zayvion dodged.

Terric pointed at him. "You're accessing magic, too, aren't you?"

I opened my mouth to argue because hadn't we shut that down? Hadn't we all worked so that Cody could heal magic, then lock it away?

No one could reach magic.

Well, except for Terric and me. And we were Soul Complements who had done some janky things with Life and Death magic.

Zay and Allie were Soul Complements too.

They, too, had done janky things.

"Well, shit," I said. "What have you two crazy kids been up to? Touching magic? Casting it in the bedroom? Naughty, naughty."

"Says the jerk who had Blood magic pens in his pocket," Allie said.

"Terric had Blood magic pens in his pocket," I corrected. "He just happened to loan me one. You dipping your fingers in the secret sauce?"

"We...have an awareness of it," Zay said.

"Awareness?" Terric asked.

"Dreams," Allie said, just a little too quickly, like this was a careful half-truth. "Sometimes the taste of it, the smell. It isn't as hidden as it used to be."

Well, that wasn't good.

Terric scratched at the back of his neck. "I've notice that too."

That was news to me.

"Is this something all Soul Complements feel?" Allie asked. "All magic users? Or just those of us who have been in magic up to our eyeballs for our entire lives?"

Terric shook his head. None of us knew the answer to that.

Zay said, "Those hot spots are bound to be found."

"What is up with Stone?" I asked. "You've got a gargoyle that's eating magic and passing it on to a child."

Immediate, matching frowns.

"Are you sure he ate magic?" Allie asked. "Or was...did he just give a little of the magic inside him to...ground her?"

"Those are weirdly specific questions," I noted.

"Ramona," Terric said, getting to the heart of what had brought us all here, the heart of why we had spilled the beans and brought Al and Zay in on our secrets. "Has she shown any other signs of using magic?"

"No." That from Allie. She glanced at Zayvion and he shook his head, agreeing with her.

"Tonight was the first time?" Terric pressed.

"We think so," Allie answered. "It's just..." She crossed her arms over her chest, her gaze shifting to the stairs, and unconsciously, to the room where Ramona slept.

"It's a lot to deal with," she said. "Knowing she could tap into it. And use it, correctly, without training."

"We won't let her get hurt," I said. "You know that right? We all are one hundred percent here to make sure that little girl doesn't get a scratch on her."

"Shame's right," Terric said. "This time."

"Shame's right every time," I said.

"We'll keep her safe," he said. "We need to find out

how Stone ate that burning paper, how he channeled the magic, and how Ramona tapped into it.

"But it might be a one time thing." He strolled over the shelves and pressed one of the books back into place. "It could be just this one kind of magic leak. Just this one way Stone accessed it. Just this one way she was able to touch it and use it."

"She didn't touch it," I said, "she absorbed it." Everyone went silent as that truth bomb exploded.

"She held it in her body," I went on, needing to make this point, "and it didn't hurt her, other than making her tired. She turned it into Light—and sure, that's one of the simplest spells—without having to draw a glyph, without having to use herbs or chanting, or any of this." I waved at the shelves.

"Theories?" Terric asked to the room in general.

"I have one," Cody said from the top of the stairs. "I have an idea why Ramona used magic. And maybe where it came from. Probably. Mostly for sure. But you have to come back upstairs for me to show you."

We tromped up the stairs and gathered in the living room again.

Stone lay on his belly with the painting on the floor in front of him. He rubbed his face across it, first one cheek and then the other, making drunken, happy sounds.

He scrabbled at it, trying to reposition the canvas.

Once he got it how he liked it, he went back to face rubbing.

Allie walked over and crouched in front of him. "What is going on? Is this gargoyle-nip? Are you drunk?"

Stone hummed happily and blinked to bring Allie into focus.

"No more taking Ramona out without us knowing, right, Stoney?"

He cooed and sat, abandoning the painting. She rubbed his head, and he hugged her, his wings wrapped around her back.

"Good boy." She scrubbed at his neck, and he grumbled, pleased. "So, what's the theory?" she asked Cody.

As soon as she stood, Stone picked up the painting again, clicked at it, and gently bit the corner.

"It's about me," Cody said. "I mean, it's about Ramona too. What we have in common."

"An overwhelmingly co-dependent relationship with a gargoyle?" I asked.

He flashed me a smile. "Sure, that's part of it. But we're both children of Soul Complements. Powerful Soul Complements."

I knew that. I mean, we all knew that, but I wasn't seeing how that added any kind of answer to our questions.

"And?" I prompted.

"And that means magic is a little easier for her to access. My magic."

"You have magic?" Zay asked. The words sounded like a threat.

"Well, magic was me. I was it. For a little while. When light and dark joined up again."

"But now," Zay pressed. "Do you have magic now?"

"I didn't think so, but I might be wrong."

I groaned and rubbed my forehead. "Cody my man. Talk simple. Talk straight. What the fuck are you saying?"

"I'm an artist, right?"

I blinked to keep from screaming.

"I'm an artist, and I've been painting. A lot. I've sold some paintings too. I mean, I do other stuff and sell it too. I sculpt, but paintings, mostly."

"Terric, do we still have those cyanide capsules?" I asked.

He just shushed me. "Keep going," Terric said. "What does your art have to do with this?"

"I think I've pulled magic into my paintings."

The hair on the back of my neck rose. "All of your paintings?" I asked.

Cody wasn't just an artist. He was making a name for himself worldwide. Art collectors wanted his originals. Galleries featured his work every time he came out with a new collection.

If everything Cody had been creating carried magic...hell.

I had no idea how big of a mop we'd need to clean up that mess.

"I...no?" he offered.

"Need a little more commitment than that, mate."

"Why do you think your art has magic?" Terric asked.

"Um...here. Let me..." He pulled his phone out of his pocket and swiped the screen until he found the video he wanted. "Remember that protest a few months back?"

Portland's protests weren't going to fade from any of our memories for quite some time.

"So, at the protest things got heated, and someone threw a firecracker. Just a regular legal firework. It landed on one of my paintings."

"What was your painting doing at the protest?" Terric asked.

"Oh, I donate art to some of the businesses who do charity work and social outreach. See? That's my painting hung outside the sandwich shop."

We all leaned in a little closer to watch.

"And that's the firecracker. It gets tossed at the wall, hits my painting. See that? Let me slow it down."

He messed with the vid and turned his phone around again.

This time everything happened at half speed.

It was easy to see the firecracker hit the painting.

It was easy to see a spark catch the paint and canvas on fire.

It was easy to see the split-second arc of magic flowing through the painting before it dripped down to the ground beneath it and disappeared.

The silence lasted only a moment.

"You're sure it's not the firecracker that carried the magic?" Allie asked first.

"Pretty sure. Stone? I need the painting."

Stone brought the painting to Cody but looked sad about letting it go.

"You did great," Cody praised. Stone rumbled, content.

"I should probably do this outside," he added.

So that's how we all ended up in my backyard, in the dark.

Cody asked me for my lighter, which I handed to him, and then he lit his painting, which could have easily fetched six-digit figures, on fire.

CHAPTER 8

"I see fire," Zay said.

We all saw the fire.

Cody had set the painting on top of the fire pit Dash had bought Terric, or Terric had bought Dash, last summer.

The painting looked sad, sitting in the wet coals, smoldering at one corner.

"That's a lot of money you're burning," I noted.

Cody shrugged. "I wasn't going to sell this one anyway. Not since I started thinking these might be part of the hot spots."

"Still only fire," Zay noted.

"Smoke," Allie added.

"Give it a minute," Cody said. "It has something to do with how much of the painting is burned, I think. I put different herbs in the pigments. I was experimenting with texture and color."

"Herbs? What kind?" I asked.

"Just things I thought were interesting."

"Things you found in some of those books in our basement?"

"No?"

Oh, that was such a lie.

"Herbs are herbs. I liked using them in the paint. It was interesting."

He was such a troublemaker.

We waited. Watched.

Nothing but smoke and a thin flame chewing its way through the canvas and pigments.

Then the flame really caught. It flared, flashing from a sullen gold to a hot white.

Neon light filled the night, and the scent of crushed blueberries and pine filled my nose.

The guitar string pluck of magic shifting and cracking beneath our feet shivered through me.

And then there wasn't a fire anymore because there was a whole lot of gargoyle chomping down on the painting, licking fire off his fingers, snarling and chewing.

Until the fire was gone.

Until the painting was gone.

Until the neon flare of magic flowed through the magical cracks and fissures in the gargoyle's stone body.

Zay and Allie both took a step toward the door, Allie faster.

"I'll check on her." She jogged up the steps and disappeared into the house.

Stone finished devouring the magic, smacked his lips, and coughed once.

"Okay," I said, looking between the glow-in-the-dark beast and Cody. "Now what?"

Cody tipped his head. "I think I can pull the magic out of him. I could probably cast a small spell? Or redirect the magic back into the ground."

"What happens if you don't do either of those things?" I asked.

"I don't know what Stone will do with the magic. Absorb it, I think. He's made from magic, so containing it isn't really that far from his original function.

"But I think just burning the painting sort of wakes up the magic in the ground? Makes it seek out the spark, the cause of it?"

"And that's why we're getting hot spots?" Terric asked.

"Are there that many people burning your paintings, Miller?" I asked.

He rolled a shoulder. "It sort of went viral."

"What went viral?" Zayvion asked.

"That first video I showed you."

"Which means?" I asked.

"Well, people reached out to me. To...uh...get my comments on my art being burned during a protest.

"And since the protest was for equal rights and human dignity, I said something like, I'd be proud if my art brings attention to the injustices in this world. If anyone else wants to burn one of my paintings to bring attention to rights of minorities, LGBTQ, women, and other silenced voices, they have my approval."

"You told people to burn your artwork? Artwork that goes for half a million?" I asked.

"I donate half of it. If my name brings attention to causes I believe in, why wouldn't I want people to burn my art?"

He looked so confused by my protest I just rolled my eyes to the heavens. "Mercy."

"How many?" Terric, ever the pragmatist, asked.

"Paintings like this? Maybe a dozen."

I met Terric's gaze and did the same math he did. We'd had maybe ten or eleven hot spots.

"So, there're only one or two paintings still out there?" I asked.

It couldn't be that easy. It was never that easy.

"One or two, I think."

"Do you have receipts? Tell me you have receipts."

"I do."

"Wondrous," I said. "We should be able to track down the ones that haven't been burned."

"And what?" Terric asked. "Steal them?"

I opened my mouth to say, of course we steal them, but Zayvion beat me to it.

"Yes. They're a danger. A magical danger. We take them off the street."

"And if we get caught?" Terric pressed. "We can't just snap our fingers and cast a spell to make people forget we've been there, Zayvion. This isn't the old days."

Zay crossed his muscled arms over his chest and glowered at Terric. "We have a gargoyle," he stated like that solved everything.

We all looked at Stone, who caught us watching, picked up a rock, and balanced it on his head.

"How long do you think he can store that magic?" I asked Cody.

"No idea."

"Is it enough for a single spell? The old way?" Terric asked.

"You said Ramona used it to cast Light." Cody pursed his lips. "So, maybe?"

"No guarantees for success," I asked. "Obvious high risk, and certain danger? Don't threaten me with a good time."

Terric was still frowning, but he nodded. "All right.

Let's get the addresses, figure out where we need to go."

"What about Ramona?" I asked, as we turned back to the house.

Allie stood in the doorway. "I've called Nola. She's going to come over and take her to her house. She'll be here in about twenty minutes."

"Just enough time for us to run down those addresses," Terric said.

"We're gonna need more coffee," I said.

"Already brewing," Allie said, as I walked past her. "Shot of whiskey by the toaster."

"You're my favorite," I said.

She gave me a smile. "I know."

CHAPTER 9

Nola, Allie's best friend, was a smart woman. She knew something was going on. She knew it was probably trouble. But she didn't ask for details.

And that is because she is also a reasonable woman.

She bundled a very sleepy Ramona into her car and promised Allie and Zay they could pick her up after breakfast. There was a bargaining moment that involved coffee and donuts, then she was gone, Ramona asleep before they were out of the drive.

Stone, sitting next to Allie, whined as the car drove away.

"She's going to be okay," Allie said. "Nola's going to look after her. You'll get to see her soon."

Stone's ears lifted, then pivoted back and forward

again. He grumbled, but leaned so she could rub behind his ears.

"It's a storage unit?" Cody asked, again.

"Looks like it," Terric replied. "Rent by the month. Which means either the painting is there, or someone is using that address because they didn't want their location known."

"Can't live in a storage unit," I noted. "Not legally. And anyone who can afford to buy one of your paintings, can afford indoor plumbing."

"All sorts of people buy art," Cody said.

"Two cars?" Zay asked.

"Let's take one," Allie said. "I'll drive."

"Shot—"

"Nope," Zay said to me. "You're sitting in the back with the gargoyle."

"Fine," I said. "Stone's better company, anyway. C'mon, Stoney."

We piled into Zay's SUV, Allie and Zay up front, Terric and Cody in the center seats, and me and the glowing beast in the back.

The address was south, near Milwaukie, but something about this whole thing wasn't sitting right with me.

"Why herbs?" I asked, leaning up into Cody and Terric's space.

"For the pigments?" Cody said. "I told you

already."

"Why only these paintings?"

"I like to experiment." His eyes cut to the side, and the tilt of his lips said he was biting the inside of his mouth.

There was more he wanted to say, but he was trying to stay silent.

"Miller, if you are leading us into a trap..." I started.

"How can you even say something like that? I'm on your side. You know I've always been on your side."

"Always? Really, mate?"

"Shame," Terric warned, the lack of sleep finally showing in his tone. "Stop trying to make trouble out of nothing."

I sat back, shut my mouth, and tried to stick my thumb on what felt wrong.

It wasn't that Zay and Allie knew about our magical secrets. That was bound to happen eventually.

But there was something off about all this.

What were the chances we'd find the painting still burning tonight when we never had seen one when closing hot spots before?

What were the chances Stone would "happen" to have stowed away, so he could eat the painting?

What were the chances Cody Miller had suddenly realized his paintings were causing the hot spots and shown up at my house?

Nothing, nil, and nada.

Someone was playing us.

I knew it wasn't Zayvion or Allie. Pretty sure it wasn't Terric, since the last thing either he or I wanted was to loop them in on this stuff.

Which left Cody.

Cody who kept sliding half glances back at me like he was expecting me to call him out. Cody who had rather easily sorted through the receipts and paintings that had been burned. Cody who knew exactly which painting was still out there.

Cody who had shown up at my place with a painting in his hand, so he could show us how it all worked.

Okay. So Cody was up to something.

Unlike his current mild-mannered appearance, back in the day, Cody had been a hell-raiser.

It was one of the reasons he and I got along so well. But back then he'd also had a gambling problem that had not worked out for him.

What I'm saying, is he was capable of getting into some deep shit.

He either was taking us on this goose chase for reasons we'd find at the warehouse we were driving toward, or he was doing it because he was being pressured.

Could someone have dirt on Cody?

Oh, yes. Very much so. Especially if he had gotten bored with the straight and narrow life and decided to go back to his old tricks.

"Hey Cody," I said. "Isn't it great how this all worked out tonight?"

Cody hunched his shoulders and stared out the window.

"How Terric found out there was a hot spot. How the painting was still there and caught fire while we were watching? How Stone snuck into my car and ate the magic? Really great."

Allie threw glances my way in the rearview mirror, and Terric, who had been dozing, straightened.

"Just all these coincidences happening at the same time," I went on. "So now we're all in one car, hunting down a painting that is not hanging in someone's home, or business, or gallery, but is stashed away in a rent-by-the-month warehouse."

Allie was the first to talk. "Did you plan this, Cody? Did you put my daughter in danger?"

"No. Of course not. Why would you trust what Shame's saying over what I said? I haven't lied to you."

Yeah, like that was convincing.

She pulled the vehicle to the side of the road and flipped on the hazards.

It was that in-between hour when graveyard shift

hadn't gone home yet, and early shift wasn't headed into work.

No cars on the road.

Allie and Zay twisted back toward us.

"Now is your only chance, Cody," she said. "What are we walking into?"

Cody threw me a look of pure annoyance. They he pressed both palms over his face and sighed.

"This is a mess. I didn't mean it. You won't believe me, but I didn't mean it." He dropped his hands.

"I didn't want Ramona mixed up in any of this. I didn't know she would sneak out with Stone. I am so sorry it happened. Anything you want me to do to make up for that, I'll do it. I love Ramona, and it scared the shit out of me when I heard she'd followed Stone."

I could see Allie and Zay's anger flash and die.

"Did you tell Stone to take her?" Zay asked.

"No. Absolutely no."

"Stone and Ramona are our problem," Allie said, even though the words were tight. "They've been sneaking out and hiding. Only as far as our yard, but we hadn't found a way to stop it yet. We thought about not letting Stone be around her for a while..."

Stone made a pitiful sound, and I put my hand on his shoulder. "Don't hide in cars. Don't take Ramona out of the house without Zay and Allie's permission," I said.

"She's not a toy you can carry around, you big galoot."

He made more sad sounds and tucked his head down, the epitome of regret.

"But," Allie continued, "Ramona adores him, and we know Stone loves her. So, we're going to set new rules. For both of them."

"You told Stone to hide in my car?" I asked Cody.

"No. I mean, I knew he'd come to the hot spot, but no, I didn't make him do anything. He likes those herb paintings and tends to show up when they burn. He likes to eat them."

"How did you figure this out?" Terric asked.

"I was experimenting with distressing my art. Things like razor tears, dirt, and small burned sections. Stone was there when I set the corner of a painting on fire."

"And?" I asked.

"And he ate it."

"I figured that, dumbass. What happened with the magic?"

"Hot spot. That first one I called you out to, remember?"

"That wasn't at your house," I said.

"The hot spots don't always show up where the paintings are burning." Cody looked out the window again. "The lines beneath the city that carry magic seem to have weak points. The magic always pushes at the weak points."

It made sense.

"And that was when you knew you'd sold a bunch of paintings that held magic?" Terric asked.

"Not really. I thought it was a fluke. But when I saw that video, and after I gave the statement, I figured I needed to try to get the paintings back.

"But no one would resell them to me." He clenched and unclenched his hands. "They set them on fire to make a point because I said they could, and well, you know about the hot spots."

"And?" I pressed.

He shifted so he could better see me. "And someone figured out what that flash of light really was. Someone figured out there was enough magic in the painting to cast a spell. They contacted me."

"Contacted?" Allie asked.

Cody shook his head and his gaze dropped. "Blackmailed. They blackmailed me. I thought if I gave them what they wanted, that would be the end of it."

Zay grunted. "It's never the end of it. What are they demanding?"

"Money. So far."

"How much?" I asked.

"A lot. I paid the first amount, but they kept asking for more."

"How long?" Terric asked.

"A couple months."

"How long?" Terric pressed, not believing that answer any more than I did.

"Half a year."

"Jesus, mate." I didn't want to do the calculation for how much money they'd squeezed out of him.

"What's the threat?" I asked. "The real threat. What are they holding over your head? That they're gonna burn one painting and throw a ball of light at someone?"

It didn't add up.

"He said he knew my friends. He said he'd hurt one of you."

"Not to be an ass," I drawled, "but there isn't enough magic in one of your paintings to do more than give one of us a headache. Maybe a rash."

"Plus, it would take someone who knew how to use magic now. The way it works now," Terric said. "That isn't common knowledge."

"I know."

Well, that wasn't good.

"Who is it? Do you know who's blackmailing you?" Zayvion asked.

"Edelman. Timothy Edelman," he clarified.

Like there was any other Asshole Edelman who would come to mind.

CHAPTER 10

"Didn't you Close Edelman, Zay?" Terric asked.

"Years ago."

"For blowing up that substation?" Terric asked.

"No, for setting up a Proxy den filled with homeless and using them to offload the price of using magic."

It was silent in the car for a second.

"How many of them died?" Allie asked.

"Seventeen."

"Do you know how long he's been back in Portland?"

"I don't keep track of that anymore, Shame," Zay said.

"Uh-huh. So how long has he been back in Portland?" I tipped my ear toward him and cupped it with my hand.

He could scowl. He could deny. But Zayvion Jones

was not the kind of man who would ignore the very real threat of a killer whose life he had destroyed coming back for revenge.

"We told you our dirty ditties," I said.

He just scowled harder.

"Tell Unc Saym all your naughties. How long has the killer been in Portland?"

Zay glanced at Allie, and she gave him the slightest nod.

"Year and a half," Zay said.

"Attaboy."

Well, that was interesting. Looked like the Beckstrom-Joneses had been keeping tabs on old Authority business too.

Pot, so very much kettle.

"I still don't see how one painting has enough magic for him to blackmail you, Cody," Terric said.

"It's not the same as the other paintings I...did more with it."

"More. As in you think there's more magic in it?" Terric asked.

He nodded. "I'd really like to get to the warehouse. If the painting's there, maybe we can just deal with it and end it."

"Burn it?" I suggested. "Let the gargoyle go crazy with it, eat it all up?"

Stone cooed.

"Sure," Cody said. "Yeah. Can we go now? We're kind of running out of time. If I don't pay him a million dollars, tomorrow—today, whatever—he'll use the magic to set off explosives by noon."

"Hells, Cody," Allie said, flicking off the hazards and speeding down the road. "Always lead with the deadline."

"Explosives?" Zayvion asked.

"Substations. Water supply. Train station."

"And you didn't call the police?" I asked.

"I thought I could deal with it. I don't want to become a target for people who want to access magic. You know what people would do if they knew I could paint magic?"

"Blackmail you for millions of dollars and threaten to blow up half the city?"

He flipped me the bird and went back to chewing on his thumbnail and staring out the side window.

"Plan?" Terric asked.

"Go in guns a-blazin'?" I suggested.

"We aren't carrying weapons."

"Speak for yourself, mate. I'm always locked and loaded."

Terric shook his head because he knew, rightly, that I was not carrying a gun.

I'd been the vessel for Death magic for so long, the

best way out of any scrap I got into was just to throw magic at it.

But now that magic was harder to access? Yeah, still not carrying a gun.

"Getting the police involved is going to be a mess," Allie said.

"We take the painting," Terric said. "Burn it. Let Stone eat it and absorb the magic. No more blackmail. No more magic for him to trigger the explosives."

"What about standard triggers?" Zayvion asked.

Cody was silent.

"Jesus," I swore.

"Call the Hounds?" Allie asked.

Zay nodded. "Do you know which substations?"

"No," Cody said.

"Hounds?" Terric asked.

Last we knew, the Hounds, people like Allie who could track down illegal magic use, were out of business.

No one used magic, so there was no illegal magic to track.

"We have Hounds?" I asked.

Zay was on the phone, texting.

"Allie," I said, "we have Hounds?"

"It's not like everyone moved out of Portland when magic ended," she said.

"That's not...Hounds. Okay, so if they're not

chasing down bad guys with magic, what are they doing?"

"They're on it," Zay said.

I snapped my fingers. "Hello, Beckstrom-Jones? What the hell?"

"They keep an eye on stuff for us," Zay said.

And oh my god, that was not nearly enough information.

"Authority stuff?" Terric asked, putting it together before I did.

Zay nodded. "They'll get out to the substations, water treatment plant, the train. If there are explosives out there, if they're rigged to trigger with magic or any other way, they'll find them."

"Dammit," I said, crossing my arms over my chest. "I wanted to be the only tricky bastard keeping secrets in this town."

Zayvion flashed me a quick, predatory smile from the mirror on his visor.

"Are we sure Edelman doesn't know we're coming?" Terric asked.

Cody spit out a piece of fingernail. "He doesn't know I know where he's storing it. He won't be there."

If the guy was smart enough to set up a Proxy pit, and smart enough to run it long enough to kill seventeen people, then it was possible he was smart enough to set up a trap without Cody knowing it was a trap.

Stone made a hopeful sound, and I patted his head. "Almost there, buddy."

Allie slowed in the gravel parking area surrounding a gray concrete building with a flat roof that looked like a hundred other industrial warehouses.

"Security cameras?" she asked.

Cody pulled out his phone and tapped something. "I uh...yeah, it's offline. You can drive in."

"Front or back?"

"I have the key code," Cody said. Because of course the little miscreant had hacked that too.

"Front it is." Allie parked the car in a deeper patch of shadow out of easy sight of security cameras.

We piled out of the car, and Cody took lead to the door. Stone galloped ahead of him, then winged up to the roof, becoming a soft glowing ball of light bouncing above us.

We fell into our familiar positions, Zayvion and Allie shoulder to shoulder behind Cody, Terric and me bringing up the rear.

Terric walked step-in-step with me. I hated to admit I liked it.

His presence had turned from annoying to something more like grounding. Having him beside me wasn't exactly comfort now, but it was a reliability I enjoyed.

Fine. I liked it.

I liked him, and liked him being around.

Cody keyed in the code and walked through.

Allie snapped her fingers.

Stone scrambled down the side of the building and hopped down next to her. He prowled into the building after Cody, and we all followed.

It smelled like clean, cool stone, like emptiness that had been scrubbed before being closed off. Like dust, and that sharp scent of industrial air ventilation.

It was dark.

We didn't flick on the lights. The magic in Stone wasn't enough to illuminate windows to tip anyone off that we were in here.

Cody turned on his phone light and muttered, wandering across the open, high ceiling space.

"Whole lotta nothing in here," I noted quietly to Terric.

"It's a flex space," he said. "Companies rent it out on a weekly or monthly basis for overstock."

"What are they storing now? Air?"

"You think this is a trap?" That was quieter, meant just for me.

"There's magic involved. Cody's being cagey."

Terric's finger tapped the back of my hand, and the spark of magic that we carried between us simmered.

It was a reminder.

He could still call on Life magic, I could still call

on Death magic. Even if it wasn't devouring our bodies and minds any more—thank the gods—that didn't mean it was out of our reach.

Quite the contrary. We could access it instantly.

That was the secret we hadn't told Zay and Allie, and one I hoped we never would.

"Cagier than just blackmail?" Terric asked.

I nodded.

"Over here." Cody's voice was low. "I thought maybe he moved it, but it's still back here."

We passed a couple doors on one side that were locked—smaller storage within this large storage—a few stacks of cardboard boxes, and a pile of pallets.

Cody stood in front of the back wall.

"Holy mother of fuck, Cody. That's the painting?"

"What?" he said, offended. "You think it sucks? It's good. I think it's good."

I groaned, because the artistic value of the thing wasn't even a blip on my brain meat.

Cody was an artist, a visionary. His stuff went for top dollar, so I never questioned if it was good or not.

"Mate," I said. "It's bloody huge."

Huge as in it was as long as the entire back of the building.

Huge as in it brushed the ceiling rafters two floors up.

Huge as in I couldn't even get a full look at the thing unless I backed up several yards.

"Well, yes?" Cody looked from me to the painting. "That's the problem."

"Because if someone burns it for magic, it's gonna burn down the damn warehouse?" I asked.

"Because there is ten times as much magic worked into it," he said. "I think. Probably. Maybe more."

Stone paced the painting, cooing and burbling, stopping to sniff it, pat it with his hands, or bump his head into it.

He tipped his head and leaped, winging up to the rafters, and landing there with a soft thump.

"Take it out in pieces?" Terric asked.

"Burn it to the ground?" I offered.

"Stone..." Zayvion began.

Before he could finish, the lights snapped on, blinding and bright.

"Trespassing, theft, destruction of property. Is that how you prove you're trustworthy, Miller?"

I turned.

A guy wearing an expensive coat and shoes, who looked like he'd been a linebacker since grade school, stood several yards behind us.

Six guys of various heights and builds stood behind him.

All of them pointed guns our way.

CHAPTER 11

Not going to lie. Staring down six guns was not my idea of a good time.

Still, none of us made a move. No one gasped, no one shoved someone behind them to keep them safe.

We'd been in this kind of situation before. Maybe not this exact situation, but out gunned, the odds against us?

Old news.

Maybe that accounted for us mostly just acting annoyed by the interruption like parents tired of the kid walking in front of the screen while we were watching a movie.

"You invite these guys to the barbecue, Miller?" I asked. "Because I don't remember there being a check box for assholes, plus one."

"I knew you'd turn," the guy said. "Didn't think

you'd be stupid enough to get your friends killed with you."

Cody tensed and licked his lips. I'd seen that look before.

It was the look that had landed us in jail, lost me thousands of dollars, and once on a strange, impromptu road trip, had gotten us kicked out of a stripper and clown convention.

"You kill anyone, there's no more money," Cody said. "There's no more art."

"You think I care about the art?"

"I think you care about money."

"How much more is a painting like that worth once the artist is dead?" the gunman asked. "Five million? A hundred mill? That's enough for me."

I didn't know who this joker was, but he wasn't Timothy Edelman. Maybe Edelman was outsourcing his dirty work now.

Zay and Allie eased back toward the painting, slow, even steps, their hands up.

Terric bumped my arm as he walked that way too.

The gunmen took the bait and moved in on us.

I moved backward, one hand in my pocket, fingers wrapped around my lighter.

If we were doing what I thought we were doing, things were going to go to hell very quickly.

I reached out for my mental connection with

Terric, lowering the wall I kept between us so his thoughts didn't constantly bleed into mine.

He was there, light and rain, sunrise and clean air, and all the good things in the world.

I'd asked him once what images he got when he tried to connect with my mind, and he denied getting any image at all.

I'd reluctantly, very reluctantly, admitted he was a little like sunlight.

I hadn't lived that down for a year, and I'd never gotten a real answer out of him.

But I liked to imagine I was danger and the night and maybe something like smoke.

I had, in a drunken moment, said so to Dash, and he'd fallen off his chair laughing.

He'd suggested, "street corner" and "stale gutter water" before I'd shoved a greasy french fry bag in his face.

"*Lighter*," I thought to Terric.

"*Good*," he replied.

We didn't share a mental connection with Allie, Zay, or Cody.

I hoped they'd be ready to grab up and throw as much magic as possible at these jokers as soon as the flame released it.

"It won't be worth shit if I'm dead," Cody said. "This isn't what you think it is."

I didn't know where he was going with that, but I was counting on that painting to be everything I thought it was: easy access to magic.

From the tension I could sense in all of us good guys on this side of the room, they had been counting on the magic too.

"Bullshit," the guy said. "Get down on the floor. All of you."

The gunmen chambered rounds, or released safeties, or cocked back the hammers of their guns.

My heartbeat slowed.

Light and shadow took on textures so distinct, they felt physical in the room, tactile against my skin.

The air was clean and sharp, spiced with sweat and adrenalin, with fear.

The light hardened, razor-edged brightness cracking shadows.

Every breath, every foot shifting on concrete, dug scars into the silence.

I took an easy breath, calming, clearing my head.

Ready for the fight.

Ready to pull on Death magic buried deep in my bones.

I wouldn't have time to draw a symbol for it, wouldn't have time to cast herbs. But I didn't need those things.

All I needed was to touch the world. A palm on the wall, a hand on the floor.

All I needed was contact.

Magic would be mine.

And death would follow.

Terric's hand shifted, his fingers finding the back of my elbow. The burn of his readiness jumped to me.

I sensed the Life magic he was about to call upon.

Fire and tinder, Life and Death. We were not afraid to burn this place down.

We were not afraid to kill a few thugs to save our friends.

Cody sighed. "This is so unnecessary."

He held his hands up and lowered toward the floor. "That's not worth the cost of the canvas. It's not even the original."

"What?" the guy said.

Cody was on his knees, but he shrugged. "You can't tell? Dumb fuck. I replaced it. Tore the old one up into bits. I've burned them a little at a time, and this, well, this is just a fake. A bad one at that."

The man didn't believe him. Hell, I didn't believe him.

"Yeah?" the guy said. "Then why are you here? Why bring this many people to steal it?"

"Because I'm tired of being screwed out of money.

I figured I'd steal this, or destroy it, and that would be that. No more painting, no more leverage."

C'mon, I thought. *You want to look away from Cody. Want to check out the big painting. See if it looks like the original.*

Another second ticked. Again. Again.

The man's gaze flicked to the wall behind us.

Yes.

Cody spun, staying low as he pushed toward the painting.

I was already moving, so was Terric. Both of us backward.

Allie and Zayvion dove to the side, putting the jut of a stack of crates between them and the gunmen.

Magic is fast.

Bullets are faster.

But a pissed off, magic-fueled gargoyle is the fastest.

Stone dropped from the rafters, snarling, snapping, and slicing.

The men screamed, bullets exploded, blowing my hearing in the enclosed space.

Stone was made of stone, reinforced with magic. Bullets ricocheted off him, sparks flaring from each hit: blue, gold, hot fuchsia.

It is not good to shoot a gargoyle. Shooting a gargoyle only makes him angry.

Stone grabbed one of the men by his extended arm, pushed up into the air with a huge pump of his wings and lifted the guy off his feet.

He dropped him down onto two of the men below. Bones broke.

While Stone was bowling a split with the goons, Cody ripped a corner of the canvas free of the frame.

Cody was cussing, or maybe chanting. I couldn't tell since my ears were ringing.

"Light it!" Terric yelled and dragged me down, pushing me toward the painting.

He didn't have to ask me twice.

I flicked the lighter lid, dragged my thumb over the flint. It produced little white sparks too weak to do any good.

Until they did.

The flame caught.

I shoved it at the painting, which was already burning—who had caught it on fire?

I glanced at Cody, and yep, he'd smuggled in one of those long-nozzled lighters and had used it on the corner of the painting.

Down on the far end of the art, Allie was holding another lighter to the canvas.

Gun shots *pop, pop, popp*ed, men screamed.

Someone yelled. The gargoyle bellowed.

I slapped my hand onto the canvas.

And called Death to me.

Buried magic, bound behind doors and locks and bars designed to keep it there for centuries, stirred in response.

Magic embedded in the painting echoed the movement, fast, eager to lift, to fill the spell I was tracing with my finger, just above the burning edge of the mural.

I wanted Fire. I wanted Inferno. I wanted Pain.

Terric's hand slapped down over mine, and the chant—his voice in my head, the words a soul song as familiar as breathing—carved the space for the magic he drew to him.

Life magic poured over me, dousing the heat of Death magic and making it stronger, like iron forged and quenched in blood.

Terric drew Blade and Strike and Pain, and yes, I could get on board with that.

I added Fire to Blade, Inferno to Strike, Pain to Pain.

Magic had rules, but they'd been broken and changed many times.

I didn't know what the price would be for using Cody's magic, this painted power.

And I didn't care.

Magic crackled under my palm, heat that should

burn but instead sent shivers across my body. It was good, this magic, laced with the paint and herbs.

It was also very, very strong.

I grabbed up a fistful of the magic, felt the heat and power of it scroll up my arm like a bracer of energy.

Terric moved as I moved.

Synchronized casting, exact and perfect as only Soul Complements could make it.

We threw that magic straight at the four remaining gunmen, giving it everything we had.

From the corner of my eye, I saw Allie and Zayvion doing the same.

Magic exploded.

Not like a firework that flamed and faded.

No.

Magic filled the room.

The color, the heat, the ribbons of glyphs hung in the air like brush strokes of paint. Chaos and magic creating its own art.

Through that wild collision of colors, poured the power of the spells.

Blade slashed at hands, and the gunmen dropped their guns. Fire burned their clothes. Strike and Pain followed.

Those were the spells Terric and I threw.

Allie and Zayvion's spells were different: Freeze, Forget, Sleep.

Aw, look at them being all non-violent.

Their spells were woven through with broader brush strokes, because the Beckstrom-Joneses were show-offs.

The gunmen—all of them—went still, blank-eyed, and collapsed.

CHAPTER 12

"They're still on fire," Cody noted into the sudden silence.

Of course, the painting was still on fire too.

None of us were moving too quickly to deal with either of those situations.

"Shouldn't there be a sprinkler system?" I asked. Adrenalin was still coursing through me, through all of us.

We all looked up. Water let loose from the ceiling, drenching and cold.

"Right," I muttered, spitting water. "Good times.

"I just love being cold and soaking wet," I said. "I just love being shot at for fuck's sake. You," I pointed at Cody, "are a bloody menace, and I don't know why we even hang out."

He wiped water off his face which did nothing

since the sprinklers were still going whole hog. "You'd have a boring life without me."

"Boring? I'd be dry, warm, and..." I heard the words coming out of my mouth.

I was about to say, "comfortable at home drinking beer and eating pizza," but that was so extra cherry-on-top of the boring sundae, that I refused to prove his point.

He made finger guns at me.

Ass.

"How are we going to cover this up?" Terric asked. "Break in?"

Allie wrapped her arms around herself. Zay moved closer and put his arm around her back, pulling her into the warmth of his body.

"Bullets and guns are going to be a problem," she said. "Investigators aren't blind."

"I think I can...I have an idea," Cody said.

He slogged over to what was left of the smoldering painting and pressed his palm against the wall.

Magic glowed soft and orange as he drew on the bare scorched brick with his finger. The glyph for Dissolve, and something that was an artistic symbol for metal and gunpowder, trailed behind his finger.

He slowly lifted his hand, drawing the magic up and away from the wall with it. He curled his fingers like he was holding a paintbrush. Then, with a flick of his wrist, he mimicked throwing the magic at the wall.

The magic splattered like paint across the bricks, rafters, and floor.

Every little droplet was nova bright, reflected like a waterfall of diamonds in the falling water before winking out.

"Guns are gone," he said. "Bullets too. I don't think... No, I can't fill the bullet holes in the walls, but the police won't find weapons or casings or slugs."

"So, this will look like a break in or arson," Allie said. "What about the rest of the painting? Oh, never mind."

The sprinklers snapped off, water dripping from the rafters and sprinkler heads.

I followed her gaze upward to where Stone perched. He was ripping the remaining charred, soggy bits of canvas off the wall and shoving them in his mouth.

Except for the ash, which was flowing with the water toward the drain in the center of the floor, the painting was gone.

"What are we gonna do with them?" Cody nudged one of the men with the toe of his boot.

"They're still alive," he said with a hint of disgust. "They know what happened."

Allie looked at Zayvion, and he nodded, even though she hadn't said anything.

Soul Complements. Mind-to-mind conversation. Handy and sneaky.

"Stone," Zayvion called.

The gargoyle scrambled down the wall, then coasted to the floor next to Zay. He hummed like a Hoover, ears pointed, neon light lining every edge of him.

"Over here," Zay said. He and Allie walked to the unconscious gunmen.

Stone lifted his lip to show fang.

"I think?" Allie said.

"You're right," Zay answered.

Mental conversation made for some weird actual conversation. I wondered if Terric and I were ever that annoying.

Naw.

"What are you two crazy kids up to?" I stopped next to Allie, my cold hands jammed in my soaking pockets. "Are you going to put these guys out of their misery?"

"Dead bodies are loose ends," Allie said.

"That's not a no," I said.

"It's a no," Zay said.

He dropped his hand to Stone's head. Allie did the

same. Then Zay stepped away from Stone and knelt next to the closest gunman.

He drew on the man's forehead with his finger, and neon blue-white magic followed the glyph.

Allie nudged Stone, and they walked a very slow circle around the men while Zay moved from man to man.

Allie's hand was on Stone, but her other hand was extended, palm upward as if she was catching water.

But it wasn't water that filled her hand, it was neon magic. The magic she drew from Stone, the magic Zayvion drew from her.

Once she and Stone had finished the circle, they paused.

Zay drew the last glyph on the last man, and I got a good look at what he was casting.

It was Rescind, an old awkward Closing spell that hadn't worked for years.

I heard Terric grunt as he recognized the move Zay and Allie were trying to pull off.

If they did it, these men wouldn't remember a thing about what had happened tonight.

Not us, not the gargoyle, not the magic.

Zayvion chanted, not his normal magic casting style, but solidly a part of Faith magic he used to wield.

As he stood, he reached out for Allie without

looking at her. She took his hand and magic went out, like a flame extinguished.

"Well, I guess that didn't—" I said.

Rescind flared blue and gold, burning with no heat, then soaked into each man's forehead like warm honey.

"Nice," Terric said. "Very nice, very clean. They're not going to remember the last week."

Zay stepped away and flashed Terric a quick smile. "They won't remember the last month."

"Month?" I said, coming up to rub Stone's ears. "They'll be lucky to remember their names. That was some fine illegal magic casting, Mr. And Mrs. Beck-strom-Jones. Top-notch criminal action."

Allie shook her head, but she was smiling too. "Let's get the hells out of here," she said. "Before the police show up."

"That shouldn't," Cody said, "Well, won't happen for another couple hours. I um..." he wiggled his fingers like he was typing, "hacked the security system."

"Don't remind me," Allie said. "The fewer of your crimes I know, the less I'll need to lie to my best friend."

"Why would Nola care if I hacked the security of a warehouse?" he asked.

We all started across the warehouse toward the door, our shoes splashing in the shallow water.

"Not her," Zay said. "Her very smart, very sharp-eyed detective husband."

"Stotts loves me."

"You've been hanging around Shame too long," Allie said.

"Hey," I complained. "Hanging around Shame is never a bad thing."

"Here we go," Terric groaned. "He's going to start making lists. Zayvion, please tell me you have a Deafen spell up your sleeve so I don't have to listen to him."

"Hold up," I said. "For one thing, I don't make lists. For two things—"

"Ran out of my last Deafen spell a while ago," Zay said, completely ignoring me.

"Really?" Allie asked, a big grin on her face. "When?"

"Last time Shame was making lists," Zayvion said.

"For things three through nine," I continued, raising my voice, "you suck."

They all got a good chuckle out of that, and I crossed my arms in mock anger.

"See if I answer your next gargoyle invite," I grumbled. "Maybe I'll just keep all this gloriousness to myself from now on."

That only made them laugh louder, the finks.

But the joy rolling off them hit me like lightning.

I'd missed seeing that in my friends.

Missed seeing their pure thrill of casting magic, of

harnessing something so ephemeral and powerful and bending it to create something new.

The heady knowledge that a single action and an act of will could change the world in a big way.

Change the world in a good way.

Locking magic away had removed a lot of pain from the world. It had taken away the horrors that magic could be made to do.

But it had taken away the benefits of magic too.

Allie and Zayvion had done a lot of good things with magic.

Locking it away robbed them of that ability. Robbed them of that joy.

And just like that, my mood shifted, and I was running back through everything we'd done tonight and wondering how our decisions would come back to bite us in the ass.

Terric must have caught my mood because he motioned me over him. "Mad?" he asked.

"At you?" I said, "usually."

He considered that for a few steps. "What are you really worried about?" he asked quietly.

"Who says I'm worried?"

"If you think we missed something back there," he went on, like I wasn't even part of the conversation, "you and I can come back and deal with it later."

"What, like a massive hot spot opening up under

our feet since we just burned a huge signal flare for it?"

I was joking—well, mostly—but he stopped cold. "Son of a bitch."

He pivoted back the way we'd come, but Cody was there, pushing him forward by draping his arm over Terric's shoulder, then mine.

"No hot spot," Cody said. "We used all the magic out of that thing. There shouldn't be a kickback."

"Shouldn't be isn't won't be," Terric said.

"Won't be," Cody said. "There won't be a hot spot. We used all the magic! All of it. And it was glorious! You saw. We did so good!"

His enthusiasm was infectious, buzzing, and I couldn't help but smile. "You are still an idiot."

"Thank you!" He pulled me in close, planted a kiss on the side of my head, let go fast and did the same to Terric.

"Here's to magic users!" He raised both fists over his head. "Breaking rules and dropping fools!"

"Was there Molly in that paint?" I asked him, but all I got were the finger guns again as he jogged backward toward the warehouse doors.

"It better be good Molly," I yelled after him.

Allie and Zay were walking close together, their hands entwined, their bodies pressed side-by-side, swaying like chain-tangled swings.

The happiness and satisfaction rolling off them

was familiar, and frankly, annoying.

"Look at them," I grouched.

"Yeah," Terric said, fondness in his voice. "Look at them."

We were silent a couple steps.

"I miss this," I admitted. "Hunting magic with them, fighting bad guys. Saving the world."

He grunted in agreement and bumped his shoulder into mine. I bumped him back.

"We're going to have to let them in on everything, aren't we?" I asked.

"Yeah," Terric said quietly. "I think we are."

Allie called back, "Damn right you are. And it's about damn time. So hurry up, you two reprobates. You've got five hours to fill us in on all the shit you've been hiding before we have to pick up our daughter."

"I do not miss the bossing around," I muttered.

"What's that, Shame?" Allie asked.

I raised my voice. "Don't miss the bossiness. You. Bossing us around. That. Don't miss it. Can do without it. Might just leave all of you and cast a Rescind on my own forehead. Zay, want to give me pointers on how that's done again?"

Allie and Zay both raised their free hand and flew the bird.

I burst out laughing.

Okay. Maybe I missed the bossiness a little too.

CHAPTER 13

We were zinging with the rush of using magic.

Apparently the price for using Cody's magic paint was a caffeine high on steroids.

We couldn't stop talking over each other, shouting, and dissolving into fits of laughter on the ride back to Allie and Zay's place.

Someone, I think Zay, of all people, started babbling about the old days, and the conversation rolled through memories of how stupid we'd been.

Of how brave, too.

I sat in the back tapping my foot and soaking it in.

I wanted to tell them everything. Spill all the beans.

Tell the truth about magic and what it had done to me and Terric, and what we'd done right back to it.

How much we'd hated what we'd had to give up:

their company, their confidence. How much we'd tried to keep them protected because they'd paid enough prices.

But I knew that just when it felt safe to rejoin a family that knows all about darkness and shitty choices, but has your back anyway, that's exactly when some asswipe's gonna show up and kick your happy sandcastle down to crumbs.

So I bit the inside of my cheek, kept my mouth shut, kept my family safe.

We spilled out of the SUV and rambled up to the house.

Allie in front, Zay right behind her, then Cody, Terric, and me, bringing up the rear. Stone hadn't wanted to ride in the car.

Allie had given him a stern warning not to fly over to Nola's place where Ramona should still be sleeping.

So he'd followed us home, jumping and crawling across rooftops, like a comic book hero.

He was probably curled up around the chimney right now.

It wasn't dawn, not yet. But I could feel it in the air, the tension of darkness slowly dissolving into light.

I hung back and stared up at the sky. Stars spangled the darkness, not a cloud to be seen.

It would be winter soon. Cold, wet, and gloomy.

I couldn't wait.

Terric's phone buzzed. He paused at the front of the porch, his hand on the rail.

"Dash? What's wrong?"

The others had already walked into the house, but I lingered.

Dash was off at a board game convention in Canada, doing demonstrations for the company who had brought him on as a designer.

The game he'd worked on was finally out, and from the stunned look he'd been wearing for the last month or so, people were really liking it.

I could feel Terric's worry through our Soul Complement link. Then his head jerked up as if he had seen something through the window.

I could feel the moment his worry changed to anger.

"No time." Terric jogged up the porch. "Yes. Yes. I'll call you back."

One word burned through our connection: *ambush.*

I dragged on Death magic, and even though I'd have to put my hands on a person for it to work, it answered, thick and hot, like tar ready to suffocate everything it poured over.

I could feel the clean, sterile, waterfall bite of the Life magic Terric was drawing on.

The wind picked up, gusting hard. The air tasted of electricity.

There weren't storms in the forecast, but this was Oregon. The weather had a mind of its own.

Terric crossed the threshold. I was on his heels.

The living room was bright, cluttered with party leftovers that hadn't been cleaned up yet.

Brightly colored toys scattered the floor, a reminder that there was a little child who lived here.

Someone vulnerable and precious.

Someone who could be used for leverage.

Whoever was here—if this was an ambush—had to be in the kitchen.

I heard low voices, at least two. One of them was Allie, the other a man I didn't recognize.

Allie sounded angry but calm.

The man sounded pleased.

Terric reached back, his fingers unerringly finding my wrist. A tap, a wave.

He wanted me to go out the way we'd come, to the door that opened into the kitchen.

I hated leaving him to face this without me at his back, but it was a good plan.

Dammit.

I spun, made my way out the door, quick and quiet, and jogged around the house.

Stone. He should be on the roof. Wouldn't hurt to add a gargoyle to the sneak attack.

I was almost at the back door and glanced up, searching the roof line for Stone.

I gave a low whistle and snapped my fingers.

A scuff of loose leaves under a shoe made me turn, but not fast enough.

A crowbar hit me upside the head.

I registered pain, brilliant and blinding, and I dug for Death magic. But before I could raise my hand, my knees gave out.

Everything went black.

Waking up with a pounding head blows. Waking up wet, face down in the dirt, with a bullet in your ribs? Oh, so much less fun.

Silver lining? Whoever jumped me hadn't done his homework. A single bullet wasn't gonna kill me. Wouldn't even knock me out for long.

Didn't mean it didn't hurt like a bitch.

I rolled onto the side without the bullet, swore and grunted until I was sitting, then took stock.

Bastard had left me where he'd jumped me, just a few yards away from the back door.

"Stupid," I hissed. "Really stupid, mate."

I inhaled as deeply as I could and pressed my palm over the bloody wound on my side. It was a sloppy shot, through and through, and made a mess out of my back.

Fuck.

I focused on Death magic.

This was going to hurt, but it'd be better than bleeding out.

I made a mental image of the area I wanted the magic to work, just to the edges of the wound.

Then I poured Death Magic into my own flesh.

Burning a wound cauterized it.

So did freezing it with Death magic.

"Mother of fuck," I swore. Because, yes, that hurt.

I shuddered and drank down the life of everything around me and fed it to Death magic's hunger.

The ground went dry. Not the trees, not the random mice and birds nesting in them, not the people in the house.

Just grass, moss, a few unlucky worms and slugs and bugs.

Meager fare for the magic, but enough.

The bleeding stopped, and Death magic didn't devour the world.

Progress.

I mopped sweat off my face, smearing blood everywhere because I used the wrong damn hand, then braced myself and pushed up to my feet.

All told I'd taken thirty seconds, maybe less.

The air was thick with the charged scent of a storm building over the top of us, and the promise that it would be a whopper of a thing.

If this were tornado country, I'd be diving for the cellar.

I scanned the shadows around me, reached out with Death magic, searching for heartbeats. The only human hearts were in that house.

Good enough for me.

I started that way, staggering the first few steps, my legs too heavy. Maybe I'd lost more blood than I'd thought.

I righted my stride and stuck a shaky hand into my pocket to dig out a cigarette. Got it on the third try and stuck it between my lips.

I lit it and inhaled tobacco smoke and burning paper. I fed that small destruction into the Death magic.

For a guy who'd just been shot, I was doing pretty damn fine. I made it up the stairs and paused behind the closed door.

I could feel Terric in there because I could always feel Terric.

He was alive, angry, worried.

Zay's heartbeat was slow, but steady. Unconscious, I thought.

Allie was awake, her heart fast, angry. Adrenalin.

The other familiar heartbeat in there was Cody's, and it was sluggish. Drugged, I thought.

What surprised me were the other heartbeats. Three. That was a lot of strangers in my friends' kitchen.

A lot of soon to be dead strangers.

I pressed my fingertips to the latch, ready to walk in and kick ass.

That's when I felt it: magic pulsing behind that door. So much of it, I inhaled shakily, wanting to fill myself with it. So much, I could taste it like honey and pepper on my tongue.

Maybe this was our hot spot.

Maybe someone had dug their way down to tap magic.

Maybe someone already had a way to use magic and was using it on my friends.

I couldn't tell.

The smart move would be to call for backup, though I didn't know who I'd call.

Well, I'd never been that smart anyway.

I grabbed at Death magic, let it ooze out through my blood and bones, then slammed open the door.

"Hey, assholes!"

Everyone looked my way.

Allie, handcuffed to her kitchen chair, Terric

standing by the wall with his hands held up, Zayvion kneeling in the center of the kitchen, zip ties binding his wrists.

Face down in front of Zay was Cody Miller, who was very obviously bleeding out, a puddle of blood growing around him.

Lines had been carved or maybe painted across the floor, and Cody's blood followed those lines.

Something had been burned. A pile of ashes spread onto those painted lines.

I couldn't make out all of the spell from here, but whatever that ash and blood was about to cast, it couldn't be good.

"Move and we shoot," the guy with the gun on Allie warned.

He'd be easy to kill, simple to drink down. Death magic was hungry for a taste of him. For more than a taste.

Death magic wanted to swallow him whole.

Only problem? Magic is fast.

Bullets are faster.

Terric's emotions slammed into me. He was terrified, and everything in him wanted me to stop.

So I stopped.

I might not be smart, but I wasn't stupid enough to ignore my Soul Complement.

The man in front of Allie looked familiar. He wore

jeans and a ratty black hoodie, but the last time I'd seen him, he had been in a tux at Cody's last grand showing which Cody had roped me into going to.

He'd introduced himself to me back then, making a point of saying his name: Timothy, call me Tim.

Shit. Timothy Edelman.

The other man in front of Terric was Ricardo Perez. I'd thought he'd been locked away for drug running a decade ago.

A quick glance at the guy with the gun on Zay and Cody didn't bring me any recognition, but from the bored expression on his flat face, I figured he wasn't getting the same cut of this cake as the other two guys.

Noted.

"Come in," the guy, the leader, Timothy Edelman said. "Shut the door behind you."

I did so, Death magic thrumming for something to consume.

If I didn't feed it soon, it would just start eating. And there were too many people I cared about in the room to let it belly up to the all-you-can-devour bar.

Terric's gaze was all over me, the blood on my face, the wound in my side, and I could see how much it was taking for him not to just swat the gun away, take the shot and get his hands on healing me.

He, however, was not as stupid as I was.

He knew a bullet to the brain was pretty hard to

self-heal, and Ricardo was watching him like he was just waiting for the chance to squeeze the trigger.

No help there, then.

Zay was the odd thing in the room that I couldn't immediately read. Why was he on his knees next to Cody?

Why hadn't he looked up at me when I'd walked in? Why was his heart beating so slowly?

I took a few extra seconds to work it out.

Zay had taken a beating. His head was bowed, blood dripping from a split lip and a cut across his cheekbone.

That blood dropped slowly, hitting Cody's blood which was filling the spell.

Zay wasn't chanting, but I recognized his mental state.

He was reaching deep, deep, tapping into the sleeping magic in the earth about to be released by that drawn spell, the burned ash, and their mingled blood.

It was like the entire room was a canvas, and Zayvion was making his blood and Cody's blood a part of the magic-fueled paint.

I didn't know what would set off the spell, but I was pretty sure Mr. Zayvion Beckstrom-Jones had the match ready to burn the place down.

CHAPTER 14

Thunder rolled outside, though I hadn't seen lightning flash.

"You're the final piece," Edelman said. "On your knees, Flynn. Hands behind your head."

"Final piece?" I asked not moving. "What the fuck?"

"Down," he commanded. "I won't be as nice as Ricky, and only put one slug in your gut. I'll just shoot her in the head."

He wasn't bluffing. His heartbeat picked up. I could almost taste the excitement rolling off him.

I lowered myself slowly to my knees, gritting my teeth against the pain of all those torn up muscles pulling and stretching.

Balls.

"Why so pissed off?" I grunted. "Some artist refuse to sell you a print?"

"You people took my life. Destroyed everything I was working for. Threw away years, *years,* and dropped me in the middle of fucking nowhere with a bullshit background and no money in my pocket.

"You take my life? I take yours. All of yours. Every one of you who stood by like judge and jury and cut my throat."

"A-minus for the mob boss speech," I said. "A crime syndicate Proxy den ain't nothing to be proud about, shithead."

"Hands behind your head, Shamus, or I'll blow them off."

I considered keeping my hands down. Give the guy a chance to shoot me, so that his gun would be out of Allie's face.

But Terric's panic, and the look Allie threw me, told me my plan was a bad one.

Fine.

Thunder rumbled again, closer.

Where was Stone?

"For fuck's sake." I lifted my right hand but had a hell of a time with my left. "You already fucking shot me. We get it. You're angry."

"Not angry. Pleased. I'm going to kill you all, starting with Allie Beckstrom and ending with Zayvion

Jones, just so I can watch that piece of shit scream in agony the longest."

"Oh, mate," I said with fake condolence. "You don't know Zayvion Jones at all, do you? Not much of a screamer."

Edelman shifted the gun, pressing it closer to Allie as if to shoot.

Allie inhaled slowly. It might look like she was trying not to be afraid, but I knew she was trying not to do something rash and stupid.

Like take the shot to give Zayvion a chance to escape.

But if she knew her man, and she did, she knew Zayvion wasn't going to run. Would never run.

And her being hurt wasn't going to tip the scales in our favor.

"Shut up, Shame," Terric said, drawing the attention to himself.

I didn't like that.

"You shut up," I said. Then to Edelman, "You are in over your head, mate. Just walk away before I fuck you up."

"Go to hell, Shamus."

The gun swung toward me.

His finger squeezed the trigger.

Lighting cracked, so bright and close, the air sizzled.

Electricity vaporized atoms.

Thunder hit like a sledgehammer, simultaneous to the lightning.

It was so loud and close in that small space, I yelled and slapped my hands over my ears.

The flash was enough to throw off Timothy's aim. He jerked. A bullet hit the wall behind me, showering me in dust.

I shoved to one side, creating a smaller target.

The kitchen lights sputtered and blew, glass shattering and flying all over the room.

Gunfire peppered the darkness and was utterly drowned out by the next crack of thunder.

Lightning stuttered like a snake tongue, slashing the world into midnight strips.

"Fuck, shit, fuck!" I yelled. My ears were so blown I couldn't hear my own voice.

I stood and dove for one of the gunmen, the flat-faced guy who had been covering Zayvion. He'd lost track of Zay in the dark.

No one was where they had been, something I think even the gunmen figured out.

Before I could grab for the light on my phone, or think of a less stupid plan, a ball of green fire flew through the doorway and spewed flames across the kitchen ceiling.

Except that fire wasn't burning.

Because that fire was magic.

It was called Wild magic, Storm magic. It was very, very rare, and was very, very deadly.

They say you'd be a fool to try to harness it.

They say anyone who does suffers.

They say it will wipe your brain and leave you an empty husk.

Well, yeah. Sure.

But they had never met Allison Angel Beckstrom-Jones.

Allie had shed the handcuffs and stood like a goddess on the mount, one hand raised to the ceiling, absinth-green magic pouring into her palm and streaming down her arm in whorls of gold.

Storm clouds swirled above her.

Her hair caught in a wind I could not feel.

Her eyes burned green.

Allie was a column of light and fire.

Zayvion rose beside her, a mountain of shadow and power, the ties binding his wrists gone. The shadow cast by magic wrapped him and carved him into granite.

His head was tipped down, his teeth bared, and his eyes burned hot molten gold.

If Allie was lightning, Zayvion was thunder.

Soul Complements could make magic do things no

one else could make it do. They could break magic, heal magic, twist magic, warp magic.

And they could call Wild magic down out of the storm and wield it as a blade against the gunmen in the room.

Allie and Zayvion traced a glyph in the air at the same time, a perfect mirrored End.

It was beautiful.

It was powerful.

It was impossible.

Magic couldn't be used like this anymore. Not in this old way.

Three gunmen fell to the ground, dead.

Stone trotted into the room, ignoring the dead, intent on nothing but Allie and Zay.

He paced around them making cooing, vacuum cleaner sounds.

Then he shoved his big wide head between them and forced them to move just that small bit apart.

It looked practiced. It looked rehearsed and repeated.

They had done this before. Maybe many times.

He popped his lips, making a bell-like sound.

Allie, trance-like, dropped her hand with the magic and rested it on his head. Zayvion did the same.

Stone soaked up the remaining magic Allie held.

He soaked up the magic Zayvion held, too,

drinking down the light and shadow until there was no cloud of magic fire on the ceiling.

Until there was no magic in the room.

The thunder rumbled far, far away and was silent.

It didn't feel like there had been magic in the room at all.

Seconds. This had taken less than ten seconds.

"Holy shit," I said, as Terric panned his phone light over the room. "What the ever-loving fuckballs was that?"

Allie scrubbed her face, tired. "That was three criminals in my kitchen trying to kill us."

I found my phone and added the light to the room.

Zayvion gave Stone one more pat, then pulled Allie into his arms. He pressed his mouth near her ear, and she tucked her head against his chest.

He said something and she nodded. After a few minutes, she relaxed against him. They remained there, breathing together. Probably sharing the pain, the price of calling on that magic.

I was watching all this and trading looks with Terric. He appeared just as annoyed as I was by this turn of events.

"So," I said. "Looks like someone's been cheating on the whole no-using-magic thing."

Cody moaned, stirred, and sat up, blinking like a mole in the sun.

"What'd I miss?" he asked. "Why are there more dead people? Did Allie and Zay call down Wild magic again?"

"Again?" Terric said.

Cody nodded, then pressed his hand on his head.

"Son of a bitch," I said.

CHAPTER 15

"How long?" Terric demanded after we'd replaced the shattered light bulbs. "How long have you two been accessing magic?"

Cody was a little wobbly when he'd stood.

Zay had caught his arm and helped him to sit at the kitchen table.

Cody had accepted the ice pack from Allie and was currently resting his elbow on the table, the blue gel cold pack pressed to his temple.

He was pale and had lost blood. I knew it was killing Terric not to heal him.

But that was something we hadn't told Allie and Zay.

That was the secret *we* were keeping.

"A few months," Zay said calmly, like this was a normal thing. Like calling magic out of the damn sky was something he did every damn day. "Since the paintings were burned, I think, now that I know about it."

"When?" Terric asked. "Why?"

"I just told you."

"No," Terric clarified. "When were you in such danger that you had to call on Wild magic, and why the hell didn't you call on us?"

"Call on you and Shame?" Zay asked, and I saw the trap right before he sprang it. "Why would we call on you? You can't access magic."

"We..." Terric stuttered. "Because we're your friends. We have your back." Terric was angry. Red slashed his cheeks, and he turned his gaze on me.

There was a wildness there. Like an animal who had been caged too long suddenly noticing the gate was wide open but was unable to believe freedom was within reach.

"Fuck," I said. "Because we can access magic too. Go on, Ter. Cody needs you."

Terric glared at me, so I walked over to him.

"He's right here." I steered Terric by the shoulders to Cody.

My touch reminded him that I had injuries of my own, but I firmly picked up both of Terric's hands and dropped them on Cody's shoulder.

"Cody first," I said. "He lost a lot of blood."

"Concussion," Cody slurred.

"Yeah," I said, "and he probably has one of those too. You got a soft head, buddy."

"So soft," Cody agreed with a lopsided smile.

Terric sighed. "Tell them all of it." He dipped his head and got busy with the laying on of hands and healing routine.

I dug a cigarette out of my pocket and placed it between my lips.

"No smoking in the house," Allie said.

I plucked it out of my mouth, tucked it behind my ear.

"So, Terric can still access Life Magic." I nodded at him, at his hands glowing blue where he touched Cody's head.

"And I can still access Death Magic."

Allie exchanged a look with Zay, then she exhaled. It was like they were hoping we were going to admit this.

"How long?" she asked, turning toward the fridge. I was hoping for beer, but she retrieved five square juice boxes with little straws stuck to the sides.

"Awhile, yeah?" I said.

She handed a juice to Zay, put two on the table in front of Cody and Terric and tossed one to me.

I caught it and hissed when my wound pulled.

Terric's head snapped up and he stalked my way, Cody forgotten.

I popped the straw off the box, tore the plastic wrap with my teeth, and shoved the straw into the hole. "Drink," I ordered Terric.

He didn't even see the juice, didn't even hear me. There was an awful lot of Life magic burning in his gaze.

"No drinky, no touchy, mate." I pushed the juice box against his chest.

He stopped, and a thin line drew between his eyebrows. "Shame?"

It wasn't a question. It was a warning.

I held the box in front of his face. "Drink, then heal. I hate it when you heal me hangry."

And I knew just how rattled he was by the whole super-powered Allie and Zay reveal, because he took the box and drank.

The box was tiny, made for wee baby hands, so it held about a single mouthful of juice.

Terric sucked it down, placed it behind him on the table without looking, and then cupped my right shoulder with one hand and wrapped his other hand around my ribs.

From the outside, it looked like an invitation to dance. Or a martial arts demonstration for how to throw someone to the mats.

But it was so much more than that, so much better.

Life magic, pure as sunlight on a spring morning, clean as a river tumbling over mossy rocks, and strong as gin poured through me.

Terric's hands flashed hot, then cold. Like mint. Like winter.

Death magic stirred, hungry for life, but I shoved it down, pushed at it until it was small enough I didn't have to fight it as much.

This was for me, for Terric. And I'd be damned if I let the monster inside me ruin it.

"Breathe," Terric said softly. "And stop fighting me."

I realized I'd been holding my breath, so I exhaled and stopped leaning slightly away from him.

This is a shitshow, I heard him say in my mind, mental speech easiest if we were touching.

Allie and Zayvion? I asked.

Him talking to me made the whole don't-fight-the-healer thing a lot easier.

My muscles relaxed, shoulders, chest, arms. I leaned into his hand, wanting him to take the pain away.

Better, Terric approved. *All of it. Cody with magic in the paintings, Allie and Zay calling Wild magic, the glyphs Edelman knew how to draw, knew how to power with blood and ash.*

There are too many people who know how to reach magic, Shame. Too many cracks in the world.

Yeah, well, I thought, catching his gaze. Those eyes were blue, blue, blue.

Life magic might add a shine, but the clarity, the real magic in them was all Terric. A man who had stuck by me, stuck by *us* when common sense and safety demanded he take the first bus outta town.

I loved him as a brother. Couldn't imagine my life without him and Dash now.

Dammit.

He must have caught some of my sappy thoughts because one eyebrow ticked up for a moment.

Well, I continued, *we were pretty damned arrogant to think we could lock away magic forever. It was bound to come back. People were bound to find ways to use it. Stop looking at me like that.*

I like you too, Shame. His face was stoic, serious. But his mental voice sounded like a schoolyard sing-song.

He was enjoying my unintentional overshare.

Shove off, mate. I made to push him away, but he tightened his palm around my wound.

No more teasing. No more taking my mind off the injury. He steadied me and gave me one short warning.

Don't scream.

I inhaled to, I don't know, tell him to fuck right off,

and then the heat, the cold of Life magic dove deep into my muscles and bone.

And then it wasn't screaming I was trying not to do, it was maybe a moan, or a sob of relief.

I blinked and blinked from the total relief from pain.

I looked away from his steady gaze, then back, and there was no judgement there, no mocking.

There was only a sort of steady focus. His attention was on me, sure, but most of it was on the wound.

That man wielded Life magic with the control of a surgeon and the hand of an artist.

I could feel my muscles knitting together again, and it wasn't painful.

I inhaled, testing the limits.

Terric nodded, so I inhaled deeper, exhaled, did it again.

What do you know? I was breathing like a real boy again.

I never scream, I finally said.

He shook his head, but I could tell healing me had settled something inside of him too. *What are we going to do about Zay and Allie?*

Hell if I know. We got a couple of dead bodies to deal with first.

He released me and stepped back.

We turned, simultaneously, toward Allie and Zay who had been watching us.

"Don't give me that look," Allie said, pointing. "You're using magic too. And don't try to tell me it's magic released out of Cody's paintings. A while. How long is a while?"

I sent Terric the question: *Should we tell them?*

His reply was swift and certain. "We haven't ever stopped."

A part of me thought that might be old news to them. They had certainly been suspicious enough lately.

But no. By the look of surprise that flashed across both their faces, they hadn't expected that at all.

"Explain," Zay pointed at the table, I suppose telling us to sit, but Terric walked over and stopped in front of him.

"Let me heal you."

Zay's eyebrows went up. "How, exactly, are you planning to do that?"

"Life magic."

"How are you accessing that?"

"It's been a part of me since..." He shrugged. "Since the first time Shame died."

Zay was very still, taking that in. "Years?"

"On and off, mostly on, yes, years. Life magic,"

Terric explained. "It's part of me now. I can't be rid of it."

"And Shame?" He didn't look my way, didn't ask me any of this.

I glanced over at Allie who was watching me. Gave her a wink and a cheesy thumbs up.

She rolled her eyes, and that made me smile.

"Death magic. Same thing. It's a part of him," Terric said. "Has been for a long time."

"I thought you locked magic away," Zay said.

Terric lifted a hand. "There's a loophole. Shame and I can access Life and Death magic, because it's a part of us, and because we made sure we could. Now that the big secret is out, I'm going to heal you."

Zay caught his wrist. "At what cost?"

Yeah, he was on the right track. Everything had a price. Even magic.

Especially magic.

"The price is I have to...tend it. I have to let it heal, let it give life. If I don't, it feeds on me. Shame said it makes me inhuman."

"Bloody weird, that's what it makes you." I strolled over to the table and sat, then grabbed a tiny juice box.

"Weirder," I corrected. "But we got this under control, Z. I kill a little, he heals a little, and that keeps all the magic happy as can be. The end. Now let him heal you while Allie and I figure out what to do with the dead bodies."

Allie's gaze cut to the floor, back to me, then to Zay. "I agree."

Zay let go of Terric's wrist and let Terric do his thing.

"So, I have ideas," I said conversationally.

"You always have ideas," she said, taking the chair opposite me. "It's just that most of them aren't any good."

I made a shocked sound and pressed fingertips against my chest. "I'm offended."

"Let me guess, dump them in the river by your mom's inn?"

"Very tradish, Allie, but no. They'd eventually be found."

"Drag them to the warehouse fire we just left and pin their deaths on the other guys who were trying to kill us?"

"That's...that's not a bad idea, actually. I was gonna suggest something else, but yeah, that might work."

"What were you going to suggest? That you devour them with Death Magic, and feed their bones to my gargoyle?"

Stone, who was sitting staring at the door, waiting for Ramona to come home, burbled.

It didn't sound like he'd mind being fed bones.

"What? No," I lied.

She sat back and tucked her hair behind her ears. "How are we going to make it look like the other guys killed them?"

"Leave it to us," Terric said. "We've gotten pretty good at this."

"No," Allie said. "This is all of us or none of us. How do *we* make this look like we weren't involved?"

Cody was still sitting at the other end of the table, his arms crossed on the surface, his head down. From the soft snores, we could tell he'd tapped out of this mess some time ago.

"First," I said, pushing to my feet, "we wake up security hacker guy. Then we drag the bodies out to the scene of the crime."

CHAPTER 16

Turns out covering up a death-by-magic crime was just like riding a bike.

You never forget how to pose a dead body.

Once Cody had made sure the security cameras weren't checking in, we'd sent the gargoyle to do a little reconnaissance to make sure the fire crew wasn't on the way.

It turned out they hadn't shown up yet.

Cody's security system hack had made sure the fire department wouldn't hear a peep about the fire or the sprinklers going off.

Lucky for us.

We carried the bodies into the place, set them next to the gunmen, who were still out cold on the floor since we'd only been gone for about an hour.

Once it looked about right, Terric got busy healing a few of the dead guy's injuries they'd sustained, which: gross.

I got busy making it look like they'd gotten burned by the fire.

It was grim work, but better than they would have gotten if they'd been on my hit list.

At least the bodies were still identifiable.

We were fast, efficient. We knew how to stage a crime, a death, and how to keep our house clean.

We were in and out in under twenty minutes.

Zayvion drove us back to his house for the second time tonight.

The conversation was quiet, soft country music playing on the radio.

I leaned against Stone in the back and drifted in and out of sleep.

The next hour or so was spent cleaning up blood, ash, and the glyph that had been painted—not burned —over the Beckstrom-Jones's kitchen floor.

Somewhere in the middle of it, Allie stopped cleaning and started baking.

Pretty soon there was banana bread in the oven, coffee brewing, and eggs and sausages ready for the pan.

"I'll get her," Zayvion said, answering a question I hadn't heard Allie ask.

He kissed her, holding his palm against her cheek for an extra minute, then turned and pointed at me. "Be here when I get back. We need to talk."

"Like I'd miss out on that banana bread?"

"I'll make sure he stays," said Terric, who had made himself extra gold-star useful by doing the dishes.

"Bye, Daddy Jones. Drive safe. Hands at ten and two, five miles under the speed limit."

He narrowed his eyes at me, then was out of the kitchen. I heard his boots on the floor, then the front door opened and closed.

"You okay sending him out there alone?" I asked Allie. "Lots of people wanted to shoot at us tonight. Today."

She turned on the burners and placed pans on them. "He's fine. Plus, Stone's following him."

I looked around. Yep. Stoney was gone.

"Well, if no one needs me, I'll go crash on the couch." I pushed to stand.

A towel hit me in the face.

"You can dry," Terric said.

I glared at him, but he wasn't even looking at me.

Like he knew I was going to do what he said.

Like he knew I wasn't going to leave him and Allie to do all the work.

Like he knew I wasn't the kind of guy to bug out when there was work to do.

Well, fuck. I wadded the towel in my fist and walked over to dry dishes.

CHAPTER 17

"Battery pack?" I suggested. "Small generator?"

Ramona Jo ran another lap through the living room and down the hall, a domino clutched in her hand.

Stone was waiting in the guest bathroom bathtub.

I could hear the moment she dashed through the door and handed him another domino for the tower he was building in the tub.

Why the tub? I had no idea.

"No," Allie repeated. She had her feet up on Zayvion's lap and was drinking coffee out of a Get Mugged mug.

"But all that energy is just going to waste," I said.

"Children are not a renewable energy source," Allie said. "My child in particular."

I shook my head. "She has no imagination," I said to Zay.

He just gave me a steady look. "Out with it," he said.

"Out with what?"

Terric sat in one soft chair. Cody slouched in the other, his head propped up so he could stare at the ceiling, hands folded over his stomach.

I was sprawled on the floor, knees bent, arms behind my head, dominos spilled all around me.

"I think he wants to know about us hiding all the magic stuff," Cody said.

"We've told you everything, mate," I said.

Still with the glare.

"We have. Terric, tell him we've told them everything. Over breakfast, over breakfast clean up, and now over coffee. There's nothing else you don't know."

"That hit list?" Zay asked.

I tried to keep it light but there was no way in any of the hells that he was going to get that out of me.

"Still got it. Not using it. Mostly."

"It's the list of the most dangerous people the Authority Closed," Zay said.

"Victor's list. That he left to me, Z. Me. Not you. Not Allie, hell, not even Terric. Me."

"Is Timothy Edelman on the list?" Cody asked innocently.

Damn him.

"I don't know."

"I think...I think you do," Cody said, still staring at the ceiling.

"Fine. Yes. He's on there, and I wish I would have started in the E's so I could have dealt with him before any of this happened. Happy?"

I knew what Zay was going to say. Terric knew too, I could feel it in his tension, and his grim acceptance.

"We need to see the list," Zay said.

Just five little words.

You wouldn't think they'd be enough to change your life, while simultaneously making you want to get up and get the hell out of there.

I thought it over.

Zayvion and Allie were Edelman's target. But that was because Edelman had known Zayvion Closed him.

Edelman might have been pissed at the Authority, but he was out to get revenge against one man: Jones.

"You know now that I have magic," Zay said. "You know we can protect ourselves. But not if we don't know where the threat is coming from. It's my family, Shame. I'm not going to let anyone hurt them."

"Of course you won't. And neither will I. No, don't push me."

He was right. Now that I knew he and Allie had magic, I knew they could defend themselves.

Keeping them in the dark was not protecting them. If it had ever done so.

Ramona made another run through the living room, laughing as I lifted one hand and made a fake little roar like I was going to grab her.

She scooped up a domino from the floor next to me and was off again.

Allie and Zay watched her with worried eyes.

Yeah, I'd be a little worried if my child had shown natural signs of being a magic user. Of seeing magic, drawing upon it, holding it, and making a spell out of it with zero training.

"I'll show you the list."

Both Beckstrom-Joneses gazes fixed on me. "All of the people on it who know you Closed them," I finished.

"You don't know all the people I Closed."

"Victor did."

Zayvion weighed that. Allie's foot shifted against his leg.

"We don't like you carrying this alone," she said.

I shrugged. Terric had said the same thing.

But I was pretty sure he'd snuck into my things while I wasn't looking and had found the list. If not him, then Dash.

How did I know that? He'd stopped asking about it.

So it wasn't like I was carrying it alone.

But maybe it was time to change again.

Time to rethink what magic was, what it could be, and who could use it.

For bad and for good.

Time to let my friends—my family—be a bigger part of my life.

Time to stop avoiding seeing them out of fear they would be hurt, that I would hurt them.

All of that rolled through me in an uncomfortable emotional tangle.

My normal reaction would be to just tell them all to fuck off. Tell them I was fine.

I felt Terric's calm and patience. Behind his emotions was a small glimmer of hope. He wanted them in on this with me, too. With us.

And if there was one thing I knew about both Terric and Zayvion it was that they would never stop dogging me about this.

"I'll think about it," I said.

Terric's reaction was surprise, then happiness, before he seemed to realize he was doing a lot of over-sharing of his own and shut his emotions down.

I looked over at him. "'Think about it' isn't yes, Conley."

"It's a long way from no." He sipped his tea, something that smelled of cinnamon and cardamon. "We'll start with the people Zay Closed."

"We might just end there too, if you keep looking so pleased about this."

"One pair of Soul Complements uses new Wild magic in old ways," Cody said, his hand making an infinity symbol in the air.

"The other Soul Complements use old Life and Death magic in new ways. I like it. It has balance. Tension."

"We need tension?" Allie asked.

"A tightrope without tension is just a rope," Cody said.

"I prefer ropes," I muttered.

"Not if we're going to walk a fine line between using magic, and not letting people know we're using it," he said.

"We? Don't recall inviting you to the party, mate."

Cody dropped his head to one side and grinned. "It's *my* party. *I* invited you—all of you—to it. Boom." He made little explosion gestures with his fingers.

I went over the facts, the events, carried the one, divided by damn it.

"You set this up?" I asked. "You decided to crack open the locks on magic?"

"No. I already told you it wasn't my idea. I painted that art without realizing I was using magic. I should have, you know." He stared at the ceiling again, seeing things I could not.

"I used to be magic. I held all of it, once," he went on more quietly. "But when it burned, I knew we couldn't go back to pretending it was gone."

He tipped his head to the side and stared at me. His eyes were very old, and very young. "I think magic is going to be in this world, going to be used, whether we like it or not."

Allie rubbed her forehead. "There is not enough coffee in the city for me to go through what we went through before. The secret organization. The backstabbing and double crossing. The fight for dominance and ultimate power."

She pulled her shoulders back like shifting a familiar weight. "That's done. We made sure that was done and over. We gave up a lot for that. Lost...too much."

"It's not going to be like that again," Zayvion said.

I grabbed for Ramona, missed by a mile, but still made her shriek and run off with her domino prize.

"We'll be the ones calling the shots," Zay went on. "We'll make the decisions with magic."

"We?" Allie asked.

He spun a finger in a circle. "The five of us."

"And Dash," Terric and I said at the same time.

Terric gave me a smile for that, and I nodded back.

"Six has good balance," Cody said. "Need balance to walk a tightrope."

"So, we're what, the new Authority?" Terric asked.

Zay raised an eyebrow. "Do we want to be the new Authority?"

"No," I said at the same time Allie said, "Hells, no."

"Good," Zayvion said. "Then let's be what we decide to be. Let's take care of magic, the people it uses, and the people who use it, our way. A new way."

I liked the sound of that. I also knew it was bound to be a godawful shit show.

But I wouldn't miss it for a minute.

"I get to name it," I said.

"The fuck you do," Terric said.

"We don't need a name," Allie said.

"Rules," Zay said. "We'll need those."

"Or not," I countered. "Too many rules ruin the fun."

"It's not supposed to be fun, Shame," Terric said.

"Not with that attitude it's not."

Cody grinned and straightened in the chair. "Maybe we start with some sleep? Get back together and talk things out?"

"Like patrols?" Zay asked.

"No patrols," Terric said. "We couldn't cover all of Portland if we tried."

"We'll have other ways of knowing if magic breaks through," Cody said.

"Like the hot spots you can feel?" Allie asked.

"Yeah, just like that. And the storms you call, and the Life and Death in them." He pointed between Terric and me. "All of that should be able to tell if magic is breaking through."

"This is a lot," Zayvion said. "It means changing things. Changing our lives."

"You and Allie could ride the pine," I said. "You have other priorities. Important priorities. No shame in that, mate."

Their important priority ran into the living room and patted the top of my head before running away again.

Allie and Zay watched her go.

"Better we're a part of it," Zay said. "To keep our priorities safe."

Allie tucked her feet under his leg and nodded.

"Looks like it's decided then," she said.

I sat and lifted my coffee cup. "To us. Whatever we were yesterday, whatever we will become tomorrow. Let's stay safe, have a little fun, and kick a lot of ass."

"To beginnings," Terric added.

"To family," Allie said.

"To magic," Cody said.

"To getting it right this time," Zayvion said.

We toasted and took a drink.

Back in the bathroom, a pile of dominos rained

down in the tub. A little girl laughed, and an old stone gargoyle cooed happily.

I didn't know if it was going to be right this time, but I knew facing the unknown with these people, with my family and friends, sure as hell wasn't wrong.

———

Want to read more from Devon?

Find her latest books and fun newsletter at her website: www.DevonMonk.com

ACKNOWLEDGMENTS

This book probably wouldn't have been written if I hadn't wholly overhauled, updated, and revised the first book in this series (Hell Bent) this year. But as soon as I jumped back into this world, I couldn't help myself. I wanted to linger a little while longer with my favorite Life and Death magic users, gargoyle, and everyone else. This book is that lingering.

Big thank-you to the amazing Lou Harper of Cover Affairs, who absolutely nailed Shame's attitude and also gave Stone his first cover appearance! Stoney! You're on the cover!

Heartfelt gratitude to Sharon Elaine Thompson who turned this copy edit around in absolute record time and pointed out I'd given the wrong part to Shame in the last chapter. Fixed, and for the better. You're the best!

To my husband and the youngsters Kameron and Mike, Konner and Anna (and little Phoebe) thank you for letting me be a part of your lives. You are the best part of mine. I love you.

Shout out to Patreon supporters: Aleta Goin and Anne Tisdale.

Lastly, thank you, dear readers. Thank you for asking for more. Thank you for reading. It's been terrifically fun to share these people and this world with you. Let's go on another adventure together soon!

ABOUT THE AUTHOR

Devon Monk is a USA Today bestselling fantasy author. Her series include Ordinary Magic, Souls of the Road, West Hell Magic, House Immortal, Allie Beckstrom, Broken Magic, and the Age of Steam steampunk series. Her short fiction can be found in various anthologies and in her collection: A Cup of Normal.

Devon lives in lovely, rainy Oregon. When not writing, she is drinking too much coffee, watching hockey, or knitting ridiculous things.

ALSO BY DEVON MONK

SOULS OF THE ROAD

Wayward Souls

Wayward Moon

Wayward Sky

WAYWARD STORIES

Oak and Ink

ORDINARY MAGIC

Death and Relaxation

Devils and Details

Gods and Ends

Rock Paper Scissors

Dime a Demon

Hell's Spells

Sealed with a Tryst

At Death's Door

Nobody's Ghoul

Brute of All Evil

WEST HELL MAGIC

Hazard

Spark

Graves

BROKEN MAGIC

Hell Bent

Stone Cold

Backlash

Dirty Work

HOUSE IMMORTAL

House Immortal

Infinity Bell

Crucible Zero

AGE OF STEAM

Dead Iron

Tin Swift

Cold Copper

Hang Fire (short story)

ALLIE BECKSTROM

Magic to the Bone

Magic in the Blood

Magic in the Shadows

Magic on the Storm

Magic at the Gate

Magic on the Hunt

Magic on the Line

Magic without Mercy

Magic for a Price

SHORT STORIES

A Cup of Normal (collection)

9 781939 853417